THE Place Between Worlds

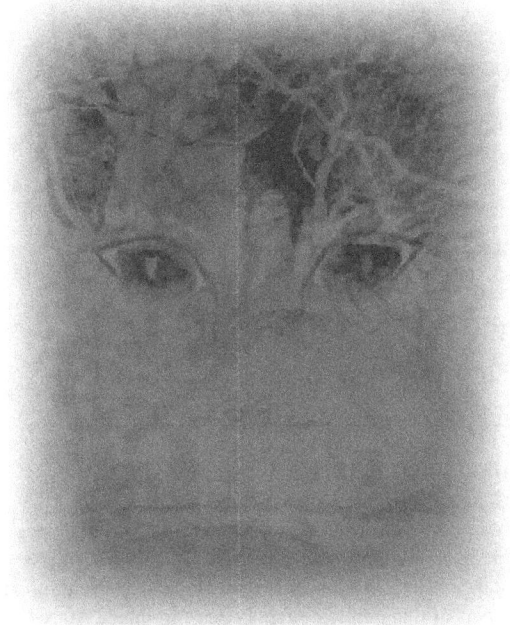

BOOK TWO OF THE WALKERS TRILOGY

C.B. Williams

Alchemy
RANCH
BOOKS

Published by AlChemy Ranch Books
4409 Lentell Road Eureka, CA 95503

publisher@AlChemyRanchStudios.com
www.AlChemyRanchStudios.com

The Place Between Worlds:
Book Two of the Walkers Trilogy

ISBN- 10: 988181410

ISBN- 13: 978-0-9881814-1-0

Text set in Times New Roman

Cover art and design by Al Williams

First AlChemy Ranch Books Edition: October 2012
0987654321

For my Readers

without you, my stories remain silent

CONTENTS

Chapter 1 - Mog

Chapter 2 - The Ancient One

Chapter 3 - Summons

Chapter 4 - Answering the Call

Chapter 5 - The Purps

Chapter 6 - Clarion

Chapter 7 - Clarion's Story

Chapter 8 - The Quest

Chapter 9 - The Searn

Chapter 10 - Hope and Despair

Chapter 11- Then Hope Again

Chapter 12 - The Power Source or the Dragon?

Chapter 13 - Birth and Death

Chapter 14 - Eaeda

Chapter 1 - Mog

The Place-Between-Worlds was shrouded in mists that swirled on windless currents. Somehow the mists moved through nothing but a damp, quiet stillness. The trees were tall and twisted, with brittle, bare branches, fingers that raked the milky mists that streamed through them. It was a dark, grey, sullen forest smothered in a twilight world of silence.

Every Walker knew not to linger in the Place-Between-Worlds. In and right back out was the best approach. Things lived in the Place–Between-Worlds, dangerous and angry creatures. Nobody knew how many or even what they looked like beyond glowing eyes. Those who lingered to find out were never heard from again.

Into the stillness came a slight, vibrating thrumming from one of the trees, causing its branches to clack together.

The sound carried through the smothering silence, as the vibration rippled through the mists. They swirled in an agitated pattern, and their agitation summoned the purple-eyed beasts.

A leather-clad leg stepped through the softened tree, followed closely by the rest of a young woman. Her thick, red-gold braid danced behind her as she swung her head this way and that, searching for the tree that would take her to the next step in her journey.

1

Her left hand held her sword's scabbard loosely to keep it from clattering. Her right hand was held up and already beginning to glow, the sign of a Walker at work. The light illumined pale, thin scars on the backs of her knuckles. Countless nicks from countless practices and a few deadly duels, the scars were the badge of a Sword Maiden whose duty was to defend her king at all costs, even her life. And there were countless other silvering scars on her body, a body that moved like water.

A tree near her began to vibrate, and the Sword Maiden whirled towards the source of the sound. Another Walker was beginning to emerge. A slow grin spread across her face, and she darted into the tree she had readied, ending her brief visit to the Place-Between-Worlds.

This new Walker was more adept. With barely a thought, barely a flick of his hand, he was through the Place-Between-Worlds, disappearing into the wake of the first Walker's trail. He tackled her as he travelled through the portal, and they tumbled out of the next tree and into their destination together. Rolling once, he straddled her, pinning her arms to the ground, his long black hair spilling around the young woman's face like a dark, velvet curtain.

His hair tickled, and she twisted this way and that to get out of its way.

"Yield, Maiden!" he said. "I have caught you, and you now are mine." His jade green eyes lit with anticipation.

The young woman hooked a flexible, strong leg about his waist and twisted, reversing their positions with one fluid motion. Pinning his arms to the ground, she let her braid plop onto his handsome face. Her sword clanked as she adjusted her position.

"I will not yield! It is you who must yield, Walker!" She laughed as he bit her braid and mumbled some retort. "What?" she asked with a chuckle. "You're talking with your mouth full, Ash. Don't you know that's rude?"

Ash spat out her braid as he sat up and gathered her in his arms, "I said, Kate, that I will always yield to you because you have captured my heart."

She sighed and leaned against him, loving his scent. He smelled of leather and rain and trees. She put her arms around him and hugged him close. "You say the most beautiful things," she murmured into his shoulder as he stood up with her still in his arms and then lowered her to her feet.

His arms tightened. "It is because I have Bonded with the most beautiful of Sword Maidens. I am inspired by her daily." He gently held her away so that he could see her face, unaware that his happiness and contentment mirrored her own. "Shall we report to the Council?"

She pretended to pout. "I think I'd rather report to our tent," she said with a saucy wink. "Or at least find Joey and tell him we're back. It's been three days."

"I do not think that there is need to find Joey," he said with a slight smile, his eyes focusing behind her.

Kate turned, and with a laugh went down on one knee, arms open wide, just in time to receive the bullet of a two-year-old hurling himself into her embrace. She stood up, happily cuddling toddler king Ioho, her own little Joey, loving his chubby arms wrapped about her neck, and round, rosy cheek pressed against her own. "Oof!" she exclaimed, as she hoisted him, "you have grown, Wonder Kid! I've missed you!"

Joey looked at her with the same jade green eyes as Ash, who was Kinsman to this king who had been prophesied for ages. "Kate," was all he said, and he smiled his joy before holding out his arms to Ash. "Ash!"

"Ioho," Ash replied, somehow conveying both teasing affection and reverence as he lifted the boy from Kate's arms. "Come, it is time to report."

* * *

The Battle Hound stood among the swirling mists, sniffing at the footprints left by Ash and Kate in the Place-Between-Worlds. A deep growl rumbled from its chest, sending out a new vibration to eddy through the agitated mists.

The Battle Hound was massive. Its enormous shoulders rose four feet from the ground, and looming another foot above that, rising from a thick ruff surrounding its throat, was a wide, square head with heavy jaws and sharp teeth that could rend flesh and crack bone effortlessly. Its coat, surprisingly soft, was a swirled pattern of greys and white, blending perfectly with the mists and trees. The purplish blue eyes, now glowing at the scent of its prey, sparked with intelligence and cunning. The Battle Hound was a patient hunter. It never failed to capture its prey.

With an deep, booming, angry *woof* the great grey beast whirled on its haunches and began running through the mists, through the trees, weaving in and out, scarcely noticing the occasional brittle branch tugging at his coat as he took a corner too sharply. As the trees thinned, he ran faster. Soon he was on a high plateau, which was barren save for the occasional granite outcroppings that jutted like broken teeth from the earth. The light was the same translucent white as the forest, but brighter. The mists were thinning as well, all but gone. The stillness remained. The only breeze was created by the Hound, as it thundered through the still air.

Other creatures lived on the high, wide plateau, using the outcroppings as dens. Some of them were predators as well, but none bothered the Hound.

5

Without missing a stride it howled, a sound much like that of a wolf. Soon, another Hound bounded up and ran beside him. Then another, then four more, until the pack was once more assembled. They ran silently, creating wind as they passed, their breath rising and falling in unison. The Battle Hound, Mog was his name, was the largest of the seven and their leader. As was his right, Mog ran in front. As was his right, Mog set the pace.

On the distant horizon was a mountain range. It was foreboding and dark, with tall spires of saw-toothed rock and deep, hidden caves.. When the pack could see the valleys and dry river beds that wove through the rocks, Mog changed course a bit, aiming towards one particular valley. They still had many miles to traverse, and Mog maintained a pace that was steady yet swift.

The plateau came to an abrupt conclusion at the edge of a 30-foot cliff, but Mog barely slowed as he zig-zagged his way down a narrow trail of switchbacks, the pack close at his heels. The footing was precarious, and they slid from time to time, their large paws sending up puffs of dust and knocking off bits of loose rock and stones that pinged and echoed as they fell down the steep embankment. Stealth was not important this far from the woods. Speed was.

Descending from the plateau, they came to a wide plain that once had been lush and verdant and dotted with the great herds of plains animals. Now the packed ground was cracked and arid, smelling of decay and smoke. The mists barely touched this area, and the visibility was unimpaired. Mog homed in on the faint trail that headed directly to the valley like the shaft of an arrow. They crossed the plain in single file, a line of white and swirling fur against the dark, thirsty earth. Even if they had wanted to, there was no place for them to hide.

It would have taken most animals two days to cross the dead, dry plain. For Mog and his pack, it took only ten hours. When they finally reached the valley's entrance, their tongues were dry from panting, their great sides heaving. They stopped in the never-ending twilight to rest and to get a drink from a tired spring that had somehow managed to create a shallow pool of muddy moisture. One of the pack dug through the mud to make the pool larger. They fell to lapping, licking the mud after they had drained the pool.

Mog lay down as he waited for the spring to refill, ears pricked, nostrils flaring. Finally finding the scent he was seeking, he let out a sigh and gruff *hrrumpf* of satisfaction. He rose to lap gently from the now-filled pool, careful to avoid stirring up the mud. The liquid was sweet and cold.

The rest of the pack had flopped on their sides to rest, trusting their leader to keep them safe. After a few minutes, Mog let out a soft *yip* which sent the pack to its feet, ready, as always, to follow Mog wherever he led them.

They set off up through a narrow valley flanked by grey and black granite walls that towered some fourteen thousand feet into the air. Had they had snow on their peaks, they would have been spectacular. Towards the end of the valley was another cliff with a large, flat outcropping that jutted approximately sixty feet out over the valley floor. This was where Mog led his pack, up ancient stairs carved into the stone. When they arrived, they found themselves on the lip of a great cave, a huge, yawning, dark opening into the side of the mountain. It was decorated with the script of a long-dead language carved deeply into the stone.

Mog and his pack sat in a semicircle around the opening of the cave to wait.

The Ancient One knew they were there. The Ancient One would come in its own time. A Battle Hound did not make demands of the Ancient One. A Battle Hound merely waited and obeyed.

Chapter 2 - The Ancient One

As Ash and Kate walked toward the Brendt encampment they were greeted with waves and hoots of congratulations. A newly Bonded Pair was always an excuse for celebration, and after only three days, Ash and Kate were still targets of numerous jokes and congratulations. When they stopped in front of the main tent, a small crowd surrounded them with laughter and hugs.

The tent opening parted and Brann, Leader of the Brendt, stepped out into the throng. "So this is why the commotion!" he exclaimed, his bearded mouth curving upwards. Hands fisted on his hips, he rocked back on his heels. "Are you needing some lessons on taming a Sword Maiden, then?" he asked Ash. The crowd guffawed as Brann's own Sword Maiden and Bond Mate yanked on his braid, causing him to stagger back and nearly fall.

"That should teach you to be rude, that it should, my liege," Lady Faith commented with a twinkle. She winked at Kate and nodded at Ash. "Welcome home to you both. We did not expect you this soon."

Ash handed Joey to Kate in order to pay his formal respects to his liege lord and lady. Brann returned the fist-to-heart gesture and then clasped arms with his Kinsman.

Lady Faith hugged Kate, including Joey in her embrace. "This one knew you were coming," she told Kate. "I should have listened to him." She glanced at Joey's serious expression. "Aye, I won't be making that mistake twice," she told him.

The two-year-old shrugged and tucked his head under Kate's chin with a grin. She kissed the top of his head, inhaling his sweet scent and smiling into his hair. "Joey knows things," she murmured. "He always has."

"So, what did bring you back?" asked Brann, beckoning the two Walkers inside with one hand and waving the crowd back to work with the other.

"We have news," Ash replied, allowing Faith and Kate to enter before him. His eyes followed Kate as she brushed by him. "Council business."

Brann glanced at his Bond Mate, raising an eyebrow. "Is that so?" he asked, sinking into a nearby chair and waiting for the others to get settled. He cocked his head at Kate. Glancing at her sword, he cleared his throat.

"Oops, sorry," she said, reddening. She handed Joey to Ash and unbuckled TinneHolm from her waist, laying it down beside her in accordance with protocol, as Ash had already done.

Brann grunted.

Faith frowned at him and shook her head, "He likes his protocols," she said affectionately. "Refreshments?" she asked, her glance including them all.

"Please," Kate replied.

"And I as well," said Ash.

One of Faith's ladies brought four glasses of apple cider on a tray and served them before quietly returning to the back of the large, circular tent. Kate shared her glass with Joey. It was cold and slightly sweet. "Perfect, thank you." she told Faith, who nodded with a smile.

"And what is this Council business?" Brann asked them both.

Kate glanced at Ash.

"As we were traveling, we came upon another Walker," Ash began. "This is not uncommon. But when we came upon her again and then a third time, we became suspicious."

"So we set a trap for her," Kate chimed in, "and questioned her."

"She was of Lophft," Ash said, "under orders to follow us, to find Brendt."

"Ahh," said Brann, absently scratching his beard. "It was only a matter of time. We couldn't remain hidden forever."

Faith nodded. "Two years is a long time to remain in one spot, no matter how well hidden we have been. Ruis is large, but not that large."

"We have not yet been discovered, although they are aware of our general area," Ash reported. He glanced at Kate. "We have devised a plan," he added.

"And that would be?" Brann inquired.

"We hide out on Earth for a few years," Kate replied.

"And you think we can be hidden on Earth?" Brann asked.

"We do," said Ash. "Perhaps not as one large encampment, but it can be done. There are enough of us here with the necessary Gifts to hide ourselves."

"For how long?" Brann asked.

"As long as it took for us to find another safe place on Ruis." Kate said. "Or somewhere else." Her eyes grew dreamy. "There are so many beautiful worlds," she whispered.

"But none so nice as Ruis," Faith countered. "Before we settled here, we looked long and hard."

Brann held up his hand. "We shall discuss it tonight with the full Council."

"Aye," said Ash. He hesitated. "I fear we need to move to someplace temporary rather quickly before a more permanent move. Although we take precautions, Kate and I have been traveling so often that our frequency trails lead in this general direction."

"More information for the Council," Brann replied. "Go, now, enjoy yourselves. You are still newly Bonded."

Faith reached for Joey. "I would love to enjoy our Ioho for a few hours."

* * *

Mog lifted his head, sensing the Ancient One's presence before smell, sight or sound confirmed his knowing. She was in his head, filling his mind with herself. He shook it, and stood, his pack springing to attention at his side. They stood vigilant together, waiting at the mouth of the cave in the ever-present, translucent twilight.

A breath of a rustle came from the cave like dry leaves shifting on the wind, a slight side-to-side shuffle of something large and controlled. The Ancient One was approaching. A labored breathing followed the rustling sounds. Then a cloud of mist flowed from the cave, snaking around the pack's paws, almost like a caress. One of the pack, the newest member, whimpered. Another shuddered. Mog stood fast as the Ancient One drew closer from the shadows.

Her beautiful jeweled head was the first to appear into the light. Even in the half-light, her scales sparkled and glinted with bright turquoise, deep indigos and purples. Free from the cave walls, the Ancient One lifted her head to its full height. She gracefully curved her long neck, the under-scales a burnished gold and copper, her upper scales the same turquoise and indigos as her head. Still she kept coming, her bulk filling the entrance of the cave. She rose and stretched her deep blue-green wings. They fanned out with a leathery rattle. Her talons dug deeply into the cave's lip, and as she pulled herself free her arrow-headed tail whipped around like a dagger, scattering the Battle Hounds.

Mog held firm as the others regrouped behind him. Then he sat, giving the Ancient One his complete attention.

The Ancient One tilted her head and looked at him through a golden eye that burned bright with age, bright with knowledge and wisdom. Were she to speak, her speech would hiss and her breath would be too hot. Instead, she rested quietly within Mog's mind. To the Hound, even her thoughts hissed a little.

"Were you close this time?"

"I missed the Walker by moments."

"That is good, Mog. You are getting closer."

"It will be harder."

"How so, Mog?"

"He has Bonded to a Sword Maiden who is also a Walker."

The frill, which usually lay flat around her head, rose in spikes, registering her surprise. She was quiet within Mog's mind as she sorted through the new development.

"A Sword Maiden, you say? This may not be as troublesome as you think, my friend. Her sword. Did you notice it?"

Of course he had noticed the weapon. He was a Battle Hound. He sent his impressions of the sword through the mental link the Ancient One had established.

"Ahhhhhhh. TinneHolm. We are old friends. Two Bonded Walkers, Mog. This may be a very good thing."

She cocked her head again so she could see her Hound with both of her golden eyes. Looking down at him from her height, the massive Hound seemed small. And of course, to the Ancient One, he was small.

"I can help you with this task, Mog."

Mog's tail thumped.

"I will summon TinneHolm. It will bring the Sword Maiden, who will bring her Bond Mate. With your pack, you will guard them."

His tail thumped again.

15

"Have a care, my Hound. Use your cunning. A Sword Maiden is a deadly creature. She will not understand you. Protect the two Walkers, but protect yourself as well."

Chapter 3 - Summons

Kate woke slowly from her nap. She loved sleeping in a tent in the daytime. It felt indulgent. She glanced over at Ash, who was still asleep. A slow smile crept across her face. It was rare that she woke before him. She was glad he still slept so she could look at him.

We're Bonded! It was a marriage, like her parents. And she was only twenty. She still couldn't quite believe it. It had never occurred to her that she would be Bonded—married!—or even have a committed relationship when she was twenty.

She'd had too many plans. Like see the world. She smirked. Now, it was more like see the *worlds*. And she was loving it. She was having the time of her life. Not only was Ash by her side, but she had a clan of Kinsmen who accepted her and respected her. Their acceptance had helped her heal, both her body and her heart.

Tears welled up in her eyes as she remembered the care and planning that Lady Faith, as the clan's Wise Woman, had put into the ceremony welcoming Kate into the clan. She had still been very weak from her battle with the assassin Straif. They had even honored her weakness! They allowed her to sit when she needed to, and she had been able to rest in a place of honor to watch the dancers during the celebration.

The ceremony itself was simple, although long and tiring. Each of the Kinsmen took turns welcoming her into the clan and expressing their wishes for her. And then, together, they mourned the death of her parents. These people, who had never even met her parents, mourned them, for her and with her. They even mourned her old life, the life she had given up to be with Ash and Joey. Kate sighed. What they had given her in that ceremony went far beyond words. What she had given back to them were her sword skills and warrior heart, her love and her loyalty.

Her first year with the Brendt had been focused on healing. It took about that long, she mused, for her to regain her strength. And it hurt! She had never been so sore as she had been that year! Even in all the years of her gymnastics practice. Again, it was Faith who worked with her, sparred with her, and then rubbed healing salves into her overworked muscles. She made friends, met the other Sword Maidens. Practiced and sparred with them as well. And she took care of Joey.

Actually, the whole Clan took care of Joey, but Kate enjoyed the most freedom to be with him whenever she could. Whoever had him would automatically hand him to her when she wanted him. She thought that it had a lot to do with the Prophecy, the part that talked about her being Eaeda, Ioho's Shield.

That first year she did not see as much of Ash as she wanted to. He was gone so often. But when he returned, he was attentive and courtly, bringing her small gifts from his travels and telling her amusing tales. It made her eager to Walk with him again.

"Aye, that would be grand," he had agreed. "But you need to be fit and strong, Kate. Even with the Gifts that come with being a Walker, you need health and wholeness to truly utilize them."

The second year, when she was back to health and wholeness, was totally awesome. Not only was she with Ash, she learned how to be a Walker. She learned how to merge with the trees and reemerge someplace else, how to aim her focus and intention to take her directly to her destination. She learned how to carry people through the portals, how to mask herself and others, and how to blend in with the new environments.

It wasn't easy. She had a newfound respect for Ash and what he did. His abilities had made her think it was going to be easy! She smiled at that thought and reached out to gently touch the slope of his shoulder. *He is so beautiful, my Bond Mate, that he is,* she thought mimicking his speech patterns. Ash mumbled and turned over, which was fine by Kate, because she loved watching his muscles move.

The worlds Ash had taken her to as she practiced becoming a Walker! Some were right out of the fairy tales, beautiful and magical. Some were filled with danger and death, making her glad she had TinneHolm. Being a Sword Maiden and a Walker had certain advantages, that was for sure. After their Bonding ceremony they had planned to spend a whole month world-hopping. Ash was letting her pick, too.

She frowned. That was probably why that other Walker had been able to follow them so easily. She was still clumsy, and she bet she'd left an energy trail a mile wide. However, it was her warrior training that made her realize they were being tailed, a fact that soothed her bruised ego. The woman from Lophft was good. But Ash was better. That had made Kate even more proud of her Bond Mate.

She also loved his playful side. They had serious matters to bring back to the Clan, but he was the one who had challenged her to a race to see who could get home first. It also made her realize he was beginning to trust her Walker abilities. It was the first time she'd Walked alone.

"I can feel you watching me, Kate of Brendt, Walker, Sword Maiden, Shield of Ioho and my Bond Mate."

Kate giggled, "Is that the right order?"

Ash rolled over and looked into her eyes, "What do you think?" he asked gently, lifting her hand and kissing her palm. "What do you think, woman who has stolen my heart?"

Kate sighed and put her free hand over his heart. "I think," she said slowly, "that you've got it all in reverse."

Ash grinned. "Aye, that I have, Kate." He released her hand and stretched, reminding her of a large cat. "You are looking so fetching, my Bond Mate. It is regrettable that we have a council meeting to attend."

"Yes, it is, Bond Mate," she replied, sitting up and re-braiding her hair. "And I'm sure Brann of Brendt's protocols have nothing to say about a late, newly Bonded pair."

Ash laughed, already pulling on his clothes. "Aye, it is best to hasten, my Kate."

* * *

Even though it was a meeting of the Council, it seemed like the whole House of Brendt was present. By the time Kate and Ash had arrived, it was standing room only. Ducking through the tent flap, they managed to squeeze themselves into a side corner. Brann singled them out from his place at the long table and gave them a nod.

The meeting was held in the Common Tent, a gathering place that was open to everyone, whenever a person wanted. It reminded Kate of the great halls of the Vikings she had read about in her history classes. Kate noticed that the large tent had been rearranged since her visit earlier that day to accommodate a Council Meeting. The rustic wooden dining table had been relocated to the back of the tent and draped with a colorful woven carpet. Two large candles were placed on it for illumination. The different sitting areas that Faith had created for the tent by using screens and arranging furniture around colorful and lush carpets had been taken down. The majority of the ornately carved and cushioned chairs had been unceremoniously stacked outside the front of the tent, underneath the huge awning.

Kate counted nearly 175 people packed into the crowded tent with barely room to move. Only the lookouts and guards were left outside, and, of course, the women in charge of child care. But not all children, Kate noted, as a small hand found hers. She looked down and smiled at Joey's upturned face. Stooping, Kate picked him up so he could have a better view.

"I just can't bring myself to call you *Ioho*," she whispered into his soft curls. "I hope you don't mind, but you'll always be *Joey* to me."

Joey smiled. "Joey to Kate is nice," he whispered back, claiming her braid to play with.

There were three at the council table. Brann, as the clan's Leader, presided. The other two were Lady Faith, the clan's chosen Wise Woman, and Lorcan, the Captain of the Guard.

Kate really wasn't that interested in politics, but from what she had gathered, Brann would always be Leader until his death, or until Ioho was of age. Faith and Lorcan were chosen by the clan as well, but they filled those positions for as long as they, themselves,

22

felt capable of fulfilling its requirements. Kate thought that was an interesting way to manage a fairly loose system of government. She wondered if the House of Lophft was run the same way. She made a mental note to ask Ash later.

Brann banged his wooden gavel to silence the room. Briefly he described what Ash and Kate had told him, along with their suggestions. "I would like to hear what our Wise Woman and Guard's Captain have to say, and then we will take a vote." Brann handed his gavel to Faith, indicating her turn to speak.

There were dark circles under the blue eyes Faith raised to look at the people who depended upon her to feed and fortify their hearts. "The gods and goddesses know I do not wish to wander yet again. There is nothing more that I want than to set down deep roots with my Kinsmen around me. But if I were to choose, I'd rather be with my Kinsmen than rooted and alone."

She paused and smiled, deepening the creases at her eyes and around her mouth. "I do not wish to leave Ruis. I will fight for the pleasure of staying on the world that we found and claimed as our own." Feeling Ioho's piercing gaze upon her, she glanced at him. "There is hope," she said, smiling softly. "As long as there is hope, I suggest we remain on Ruis, and find another place to hide."

Lorcan reached for the gavel, but Faith held up her hand. "I feel the suggestion of several encampments is a good one. There will be fewer of us for defensive purposes, but we will be easier to hide."

Then she handed the gavel to Lorcan. Brushing a few stay strands of her silvery hair from her face, she settled back and watched as the Kinsmen whispered to one another. Lorcan pounded the gavel once and the murmuring ceased.

"Good people," began the large, bear-like man. "It will not be easy, especially with winter so soon upon us, but yes: more encampments and deeper into the mountains. With our backs against cliffs, we can create quite a snug defense for ourselves." He handed the gavel back to Faith, who handed it to her Bond Mate.

"And it is my opinion that we do as Lorcan suggests," began Brann. "There will be a need for much organization, especially since the game, our food source, will be coming back down from the high places. We will need to make use of all our Gifts." He sat back, bracing both hands on the table. "Are there any comments before we take the matter to vote?"

There were no comments, and the unanimous decision was that it was critical to move deeper into the mountains as three encampments. Brann excused the clan, telling them that the Council would set a plan in motion.

"We're going to need our Walkers," Brann said to Kate and Ash as clan members emptied the tent. "So you two stay close."

Kate looked at Ash. "So much for our honeymoon," she said with a sigh.

"Tis only been delayed," he replied with a smile as they went to join the throng exiting the tent.

"That was a quick Council," Ash commented as he trailed out behind Kate, who still carried Joey.

Kate nodded. "Do you think it was because it was getting so hot in there with all the bodies?" She fanned herself. "I was burning up." Glancing at Joey, she laughed. "Look at Joey, his hair is wet!"

Ash grinned. "We will be cooling off soon." His breath looked like steam. "I believe we will be seeing our first frost tonight."

Kate nodded, putting Joey's collar up around his neck. "Shall we eat together before we take Joey back to the sleeping tent?" It wasn't a normal clan thing, to bundle all the children in one place for sleeping. But during the years that the Brendt had been on the run, it seemed the best way to protect them. Kate thought it was a good way for Joey to make friends, although a part of her wished for a family life for him with Mr. and Mrs. Sullivan. But then the life she was imagining for Joey wasn't his destiny. He never had been Joey Sullivan of Earth.

That night, her sword began to glow.

Chapter 4 - Answering the Call

Kate nearly bumped into Lady Faith as the clan Wise Woman came running out of the cook tent, head down, greying hair spilling over her forehead and into her eyes. She glanced up from her list and shook away the obstructing strands just in time to see Kate's surprised expression as she side-stepped around the girl. "Blessings to you, Kate! Busy day," she said as she hurried past and into the bustling camp.

The Brendt encampment looked like a disturbed anthill, with intent and focused people scurrying this way and that.

"Wait! Faith! I was looking for you," Kate called, hurrying to catch up to the whirlwind of a woman on a mission.

"No time," the whirlwind answered. "Walk with me Kate. There's much to do if we're to break camp in a week's time."

Kate's eyes widened. "*A week*? But we just decided to move last night."

Without pausing, Faith shot a sideways glance at the young woman, "Once the Brendt make a decision, we act." she said with a grin. "No moss to gather on our backsides, to be sure! So, come with me to supervise the dividing of the provisions and tell me why you're looking for me."

"It's about this," she answered, holding up her sword wrapped in a blanket. "TinneHolm's acting weird."

"Weird? What does that mean?" Faith chuckled. "The words that come out of your mouth, sometimes, my girl."

"Strange," Kate replied, hurrying to catch up again. *The woman sure could hustle when she wanted to*, she thought. "It's glowing."

Faith stopped short and turned, forcing the girl to take a backwards hop. "Did you say it's glowing?"

Kate nodded. "And it gets brighter in some directions and dimmer in others. It's just…weird."

Faith drew Kate out of the bustle of the camp, between two tents. "Show me."

Kate withdrew her sword from the blanket and held it up to her fellow Sword Maiden.

Faith's lips parted slightly as she reached out as if to touch the sword. But of course, she did not actually touch it. No Maiden would ever touch another's sword. "A summoning!" the older woman whispered. "By the gods and goddesses of light and shadow, I never would have dreamed I would have lived to see an actual sword summoning."

Kate shot her a questioning glance when she heard the reverent tones. "What does it mean?"

Faith's excited face reflected the glow of the still-scabbarded sword. "I do not believe what my eyes are seeing," she whispered. "Kate, your sword is being *summoned*!"

"Okay-y-y," Kate replied slowly. "But what does that *mean*?"

"It means, my girl, that an Ancient One still lives."

"An Ancient One?"

"Yes, One who has been since the beginning, the dawn of our whole existence. They are beyond myth and legend, Kate. They…" The older woman paused, tears in her eyes. "They wrote the book of Phagos, our holy book. The book of the Prophecy. We have thought they were long gone. Dust. Yet, your sword is being summoned." She touched Kate on the shoulder. "Go."

"What?"

"Go. Gather your belongings and follow your sword. Now."

"But—" Kate, shook her head in bewilderment. "Can't this wait? The Walkers are needed to find the new camps."

"Ash can do that. You are a Sword Maiden first, Kate. You duty is to your King, and to your sword, in that order. Everything else is secondary to those two covenants. You *must* follow your sword, Kate. You know this."

Kate gathered TinneHolm in its blanket and cradled her glowing Sword Ally to her chest. "I do know this," she said, head bowed. "I'll say good-bye to Ash and Joey."

Faith put a strong arm around the young woman's shoulders, giving them a squeeze. "Above all things, Kate, trust your sword. You know this as well—your sword will keep you safe."

"I will, I do," Kate replied. "It's just so sudden."

Faith chuckled. "I suppose that is why they are called summonings."

Kate grimaced. "I suppose."

"May blessings from the Shining Ones rain down upon you, Kate. If I could, I'd go with you."

I wish she could, Kate thought, feeling suddenly alone.

* * *

"She told me to follow my sword," Kate explained. "I have to go. Now."

Ash shook his head. "Life does not seem to wait for us, love, does it not?" he said with a quiet smile. His eyes were sad. "I do not like you being without me."

Kate paused from her packing and hugged him hard. "Oh Ash! I do not like you being without *me!* This is so unfair!"

His arms encircled her. "We are Bonded, and I will always know if there is a great need, Kate," he said into her hair.

Kate leaned into him.

"We Walkers are never far from one another," he added.

She smiled as she inhaled the rich, spicy wood scent that was Ash. "I know, Ash. It makes me feel brave."

"You are brave. Come, let me help you," he said, dropping his arms. "I'll hold open your pack while you put what you need in it. Travel light. You're a Walker, now. Wherever you find a tree, you can just step through and get what you need."

Kate grinned. "That's a good thing, because I don't think you'll fit into my pack."

* * *

"Just following my sword," Kate muttered to herself. "Don't mind me, I'm just following my sword." Her boots crunched down a dusty path on a lovely autumn day, the kind where the sky was cobalt blue and cloudless. The weather was brisk enough that she was glad she had packed extra layers, despite the fact it made her pack heavier.

It had been about two hours since she had hugged Joey and Ash goodbye. TinneHolm's bright light was holding steady, a beacon in her hand, and all was quiet, save the occasional buzz of an insect.

She felt strange. This was the first time in two years she had been on her own, really on her own. No one seemed too worried about her, she recalled, when she said her good-byes to Brann, Faith and a few others. After all, she was a Sword Maiden and a Walker. Individuals who were either of those two things were known to just take off from time to time. But Kate never had, and it made her feel strange—a little nervous, a little lonely, and a lot excited.

Of all the swords, *hers* was the one summoned! She had no idea what it all meant but, seeing how impressed Faith had been had impressed her. It also made her wish she had asked the Wise Woman more questions about the Ancient Ones and what she should expect. Like, just how ancient was an Ancient One? And was there a certain way of addressing them? Did one kneel or bow in their presence? Say special words? What did you call them? *O Ancient One?*

Kate grinned. "Now, I'm just getting silly," she said, glad no one was reading her thoughts just then. "I suppose I'll find out soon enough," she told her sword since there was no one around. "I don't suppose you care to inform me how long we've got until I do find out, do you?"

As expected, the sword did not answer. But it did glow just a little brighter, and she found that it had aimed her toward a tree, an Ash tree. *How fitting*, she thought. "Well, I guess the Ancient One isn't living on Ruis," she said, as she prepared herself to Walk.

The portal opened and she slipped through, deciding that since this was only her second solo trip through the Place-Between-Worlds, she would just go on to the next tree, and out of the Place-Between-Worlds as quickly as possible.

Only that wasn't what happened.

Chapter 5 - The Purps

The Ancient One had directed Mog to the exact tree where the Walker would be coming through.

Mog was prepared.

Kate was not.

The moment she stepped into the Place-Between-Worlds, she sensed that something was not as it should be. There was a sudden rush of adrenaline, and she thanked her lucky stars that TinneHolm was already in her hand. With the other hand, she whipped off the scabbard, and as TinneHolm glowed even more brightly, she flowed into *mugamae,* the stance of nothingness.

She waited.

At first she heard nothing other than the ringing in her ears. The mists, thicker than usual, seemed to have dampened any other sounds. They had also blinded her to any movement until it was nearly too late.

The glowing purple eyes gave it away. Kate focused upon them, keeping her sword between herself and the eyes. She felt the creature's growl in her chest before she heard it. And as it stepped out of the mists, her eyes widened and her mouth went dry.

Time to go!

She turned toward the closest tree, dividing her attention between the creature and opening a portal. Only her path was blocked by another of the huge, dog-like creatures. This one seemed even larger than the other, the size of a grizzly bear, she figured.

"Shit!" she exclaimed as she turned back to the tree she'd emerged from, only to find that tree guarded as well by yet another of the creatures. More emerged until she counted seven. Seven purple-eyed beasts.

"So I guess it's a fight, then," she told them calmly. She waited to see what they would do. To her surprise, they did nothing, just watched her warily with their bright purple eyes, giving her a chance to study what she was up against.

They were frightening, no doubt about that, with their huge muscled necks and jaws covered with the swirling grey fur that blended so well with the mists. The furry body and ruff were the same color as the head, but the difference in the fur made them creepily laughable, as if some mad scientist had taken a head off of a mastiff and stuck it onto a bear, adding huge lion paws just for fun.

Since the creatures would not make the first move, Kate decided it was up to her to begin. Her sword was being summoned, and the purple-eyed monsters were in the way of her sword's mission. With the grace born of constant practice, Kate swung her sword up into a *kurai tachi* and brought it down upon the head of the beast blocking her from going forward.

The beast did nothing to defend itself, and part of her regretted killing the ugly, magnificent thing.

But it was too late, her sword was already moving towards its target.

Only, it didn't.

At the very moment TinneHolm should have stuck the beast down, it shifted in her grip so that it merely smacked the animal on the side of its head, leaving both Kate and her prey momentarily stunned.

"Wha—?" Kate gaped. A Sword Ally allowed the Maiden to fight her own battles unless she was out-skilled. Then it would come to life and support her and guide her moves. Fighting seven ugly large beasts was not beyond Kate's skill. So why, she wondered, did TinneHolm prevent her from making the kill?

Out of the corner of her eye, Kate caught a movement, and she turned in preparation for an attack from that direction. But the movement she caught turned out to be the massive beast sitting down. And, to her surprise, all the others sat as well.

For a few moments Kate stood tensely, ready for an attack. But the beasts did nothing but sit and watch her with their purple, glowing eyes.

"What is going on here?" Kate asked the largest beast, and apparently, the pack leader.

The large beast opened its huge jaws in what very well could have been a grin.

Impossible, Kate thought, raising an eyebrow.

Keeping its purple gaze upon her, the beast slowly rose, and began to walk into the woods, all but disappearing into the mists. It paused, came back a few paces, and repeated the process.

"You want me to follow you," Kate said flatly.

The beast grinned and *woofed*.

"I'm not sure I want to follow you." she told it.

It sat and watched her as she glanced at the rest of the pack. They had remained in their places, blocking her escape routes.

She made a move to attack the nearest beast. It did nothing, and even before she stopped her attack, she felt the familiar energy *buzz* that signaled TinneHolm's involvement in a battle. *My sword does not want me to fight these things!* she decided.

With a sigh, Kate lowered her sword. Keeping her eye on the leader, she bent down and retrieved the scabbard where she had flung it and re-sheathed TinneHolm. But she held onto it, maintaining her guard.

"Okay, Big Guy, take me to your leader," she said, wondering how in the world she was going to escape.

* * *

Mog immediately liked the little Maiden and was glad that he did not have to take steps to overpower her. Seeing that she would follow, he led the way, with his pack flanking the Maiden to prevent escape. He set a fast walking pace, relieved that the Maiden's long legs could keep up. He sensed that the Ancient One was impatient to speak with the Walker who would follow the Maiden. To Mog's mind, the faster he brought the Maiden to the Ancient One, the sooner the Walker would arrive.

He took the usual pathways as they wended their way in silence through the trees. As the trees thinned out, he felt the girl's reluctance to go forward, and he was puzzled until he remembered that she needed the trees to escape. Good for him, bad for her.

The trees were all but gone when the Maiden made her move.

A yip of surprise from the pack alerted Mog. He turned just in time to see her vault over one the smallest of his group and race swiftly toward a tree. The portal was already forming as he reached her, latching his heavy jaws upon her backpack and throwing her off her feet. She landed in a heap between his paws. Mog bent down to sniff her and, despite his normal reserve, he licked her face before stepping back to allow her the room to rise.

"I had to try," she told him as she cautiously rose, dusting off her backside and wiping her face with the back of her shirted arm, hand still fisted about her sword.

Mog grinned at her. He liked the little Maiden all the more.

* * *

Kate sighed. As they walked the high plateau, the trees long gone, she could do nothing but go with her escort and hope there would be more trees before they arrived at their unknown destination. Bleakly she looked about her, taking in the dust, the thinning mists and the jagged outcroppings. A memory tickled her awareness. Something was familiar about this plateau, yet she couldn't remember why, unless it was because it reminded her of her trip through the Mohave Desert on the way to the Grand Canyon, minus the heat.

No, it was not hot. Neither was it cold. They were still traveling within the never-changing Place-Between-Worlds. And if she ever got back home, she would have quite an adventure to tell. To think! She actually knew what the purple-eyed creatures looked like! Not only that, she knew they were intelligent, not the mindless killers all Walkers were taught to believe.

But were the Purps, as she decided to call them, friend or foe? Kate was undecided. Right now, they were still in the foe category, because she was definitely a captive, and they were definitely taking her someplace she did not want to go. She would be trying to escape again, that much was certain. She just needed some trees. And a little cooperation from TinneHolm.

She glanced at her sword, and her eyes widened. The sword was glowing even more brightly. Apparently the Purps were taking TinneHolm where it wanted to go. Did the Purps belong to the Ancient One? Perhaps that is why her sword refused to help her fight them. *Trust your sword,* Faith had told her. Well, there wasn't much else she could do.

An abrupt hiss and clacking sound quickly yanked Kate from her thoughts. They were passing by one of the huge outcroppings, and the sound was coming from there. Memory hit her like a slap. This was where they had Walked the day Ash had taken them through the rock fireplace in her home back on Earth! The day she found out Straif had murdered her parents.

"Oh no," she said, bracing herself, grateful for her sword and, yes, even grateful for the Purps surrounding her. Right before Ash had opened the portal that day two years ago, she had seen what made that hiss. The huge mandibles were what Kate had remembered, black and shiny like the outcropping, and here it was again—the scorpion-like insect that stood nearly as high as the Purps—all claws and stinging tail and clickity-clackity feet as it dashed to and fro along the rock ridges.

But the Purps seemed unconcerned as one fell back and answered the challenge of the scorpion-thing while the remaining pack continued with the set pace. Kate had to keep turning her head, almost stumbling, so she could watch the battle.

It didn't last very long.

The scorpion-thing struck first with its tail. The Purp caught it neatly with a back paw, plunging the tail harmlessly into the dirt and holding it there. Simultaneously, the Purp allowed the thing to pinch it, both claws buried deep into the thick fur, fur so thick that the pincers obviously found no flesh. The Purp then opened its mouth, unnaturally wide—the jaw had come unhinged like a python's, exposing dozens of long, sharp teeth—and bit the head off of the scorpion-thing, giant mandibles and all.

Kate gasped, then tripped, taking a few stumbling steps to catch herself.

The lead Purp grinned at her.

The pack came to the edge of a cliff and paused, waiting for Scorpion Killer to catch up. It arrived while still crunching up and swallowing its snack.

Kate looked out across the wide, barren plain to the far distant mountain range.

"We have to go there?" she said to nobody in particular. TinneHolm glowed brightly. She experimented and turned the sword in different directions. It dimmed, and only brightened when it was pointed toward the distant mountain range. "We have to go there," Kate sighed, but then brightened, thinking perhaps there would be trees in the mountains.

In silence, the group made its way carefully down the precariously narrow switchback trail. The thick dust caused Kate to sneeze and her eyes to water. The Purps occasionally coughed. But even when they reached the bottom, the Purps proceeded without a break.

With the fast pace and the distances they had crossed, Kate began to seriously consider using TinneHolm as a walking stick. She knew she was in the best shape she had ever been, but the miles covered were beginning to take their toll. She was going to need to rest soon.

Apparently, resting soon was not on the Purps' agenda. Several miles later, Kate abruptly stopped, so suddenly that the Purp behind nearly ran into her.

"I need to rest," she croaked at the leader when his mammoth head swiveled around to see what had happened. Her mouth was so parched from the dust she had been swallowing, she was surprised she could even get the words out.

The Purps sat in formation and watched as she buckled TinneHolm about her waist and slid her pack off her sweaty back. The sudden coolness was a relief. Rummaging around in her pack, she found her water bottle and took a swallow. "Ahh, that's good," she murmured, a little less hoarse already, before taking another gulp.

She glanced at her entourage. The pack looked as thirsty as she had been. With a shrug, she made an offering gesture to the leader. His ears pricked up, forcing a laugh from Kate. "You look like a big old dog begging for scraps," she told him. "Maybe you're not as scary as I thought you were." She remembered the scorpion thing. "No, you're still scary," she told him as she tilted a little water into his mouth, being careful so he wouldn't choke.

The leader's tail thumped.

"You're welcome," Kate said, glancing around at the other Purps. "Anyone else?" she asked, waving the bottle.

Six other tails thumped.

Grinning, Kate poured a little water into each of their mammoth mouths before putting the bottle away and pulling out a package of dried meat.

Nostrils flared, ears pricked, and tails thumped.

Kate laughed.

"I've suddenly become very popular," she said, tearing off bits of meat and tossing them to each of the Purple-Eyed beasts.

She shuddered at the sound of their jaws snapping shut.

"Ai! Yi! Yi!" Kate said. "I hope to never get on your bad side," she told them as she put the food away, then slung the pack once more onto her back.

She surveyed her surroundings as she stood thoughtfully chewing her own piece of dried meat. At first glance, the cracked ground and dead growth spoke of drought and famine. But upon closer inspection, she noticed how charred some of the dirt looked and how some of the ground was smooth and shiny, as if melted wax from some giant candle had been poured onto it. *What had happened here long ago?*

Kate's curiosity flared as the group began to trot once more toward the mountains. She started to pay more attention to her surroundings, not that there was much to pay attention *to*, just miles and miles of emptiness that made one feel hopeless and lost. A wasteland.

At least the plateau had the horrible scorpion things, and, judging by the Purps' camouflage patterns on their coats, the trees and mists had Purple-Eyes living amongst them. She glanced at the mountains they were steadily approaching. What lived there?

Time drifted as they kept on with their relentless progress toward the mountains. Kate had no idea how far she had walked, or for how long. The forever translucent twilight made it impossible to gauge. All she knew was that she was stumbling more and more on legs that felt like rubber.

She stopped again. "I need to sit," she told the leader when he looked at her.

But the Purp had other plans.

Kate yelped as he grabbed the back of her jerkin between his teeth and flung her across his large back. She grabbed fistfuls of his soft, thick, wooly-smelling fur and struggled to swing her tired leg astride as her mount stood patiently waiting for her to settle herself. The thickness of his fur pillowed her backside, and she relaxed into the softness, feeling his powerful muscles bunching when he moved forward again, and their pace quickened. The backpack bounced up and down with the rhythm, TinneHolm jingled at her side. Kate nodded to herself. *Not a bad way to travel*, she thought, letting the breeze they were creating dry her sweaty face.

The pace had been set, and the Purp Eyes kept such a consistent tempo that her thoughts began to wander and her head began to nod. Kate was so tired! She had no idea how long they had been crossing the decimated landscape. The only way she knew they were making progress was that the mountains begin to fill the horizon. But how much longer it would take was anyone's guess.

Was she frightened? Not as long as she had her sword. But she was lonely. She missed Ash. It ached. With a sigh, she laid her cheek on the Purp Eye's fur and rested.

She woke up when she hit the ground and the wind was knocked out of her.

Slowly, Kate stood up, rubbing the side where she landed, grateful she hadn't fallen on TinneHolm.

The Purple-Eyes had all stopped, and the leader came over and licked her face. His tongue was so large it covered her from cheek to cheek as he swiped it from her chin to her forehead. She felt like she was going through a car wash in a convertible. "Geez!" she exclaimed, wiping off her face. "Gross."

Confirming she was okay, the Purp picked her up again by her jerkin and flung her on his back.

Kate landed with an "Ooof." She hoisted herself the rest of the way and settled in, making sure her backpack and sword were still where they were supposed to be.

She looked up at the waiting Purple-Eyes. She could swear they were laughing at her. It didn't put her in the best of moods.

"Okay," she said sourly. "I'm ready."

They took off, running faster than they had before, a ground-eating gait. Glancing ahead, her eyebrows shot up. The mountains looming above had totally blocked out the sky. They were nearly there! She must have slept longer than she thought. But she was glad. Aside from her rude awakening, she felt much better, not nearly so lonely or depressed.

But she was hungry and thirsty.

And she was sick of traveling.

Chapter 6 - Clarion

In the pitch dark of the cave, the Ancient One opened her eyes, sensing TinneHolm drawing near. She thought back on the sword's birth. All of the Maidens' swords were born of dragon fire and gifted with life by dragon magic. TinneHolm was the last, and perhaps, the dragon thought modestly, the best. The sword had a fierce loyalty strongly embedded within its metal. And, since like attracted like, the Maiden who was its Ally would be as loyal.

The Ancient One sighed, feeling her age and waning power, the causes of her desperation. She missed her Company, for that is what they had called themselves—a Company of Dragons. Others called them the Ancient Ones. And ancient she was. Her body should be dust by now. It was only her will that kept her as she was. Will and her vanity. She snorted, a trail of mist floating out of her nostrils. Her vanity demanded she maintain her beauty, although it took energy that perhaps should have been used elsewhere.

With a shake of her head that rattled her fringe spikes, Clarion, the Ancient One, the last of the Company, prepared to receive her guests.

* * *

Kate sat on a charred rock, combing her fingers through her hair as she watched the Purp-Eyes muddying up the spring with their paws. Undone, her hair fell nearly to her waist. She decided she should probably have trimmed it, but she just hadn't gotten around to it. The problem was that she just didn't remember about trimming it at the right time.

Looking about her, she saw, with a sigh, that the only trees were burned-out husks and stumps. She wasn't sure if they would work as portals, but she would try as soon as TinneHolm reached its destination and accomplished its task. From the way the sword was shining, she knew it would be soon.

While she re-braided her hair, Kate glanced at the sword waiting beside her. It was actually pulsing, its excitement palpable. *Interesting*, she mused.

Done with the braid, Kate bent over her legs, stretching out her tightened hamstrings. It felt good to be still and to rest. She noticed that the Purps, who had finished drinking, were all flopped on their sides, sprawled lumpily over twisted dead roots and stones. The Purp leader was alert and upright. She wondered if it ever rested. Surely it was as tired as the rest of the group.

Kate was just about to rummage around in her pack for some food when the leader gave a low *woof*. In an instant, the rest of the Purps were on their feet. Sighing, Kate refastened her pack and slung it onto her back. Bending over, she lifted TinneHolm from its resting place. She didn't bother to fasten it to her waist. Instead she carried it, thumb over its *tsuba* so the sword wouldn't fly out of the scabbard.

The group moved up the valley floor in the formation Kate had long gotten used to: the leader in front with the others flanking her and bringing up the rear. They still didn't trust her. How could they know that, because of her sword's behavior, there was no way she would try to escape? In fact, she doubted TinneHolm would even let her. Besides, now that she was about to meet an Ancient One, she really didn't want to.

The ascent was difficult. They had to pick their way through and around rockslides of huge boulders. Kate kept her head bent, focused on her footing, mindful of how easy it would be to twist an ankle. Occasionally she looked up to see where they were heading. The towering cliffs, appearing black in the twilight, seemed a warning to go back. Her booted foot faltered and she refocused on her climb, listening to the pants and scrambling of her entourage.

In time, she noticed that the ever-present mists were slowly thickening and swirling about her legs, torso and TinneHolm, blanketing the sword's light. She felt a bit unsettled and, glancing up, she suddenly felt even more so. Above them was a lip of rock that jutted out and over the valley floor. From where she stood, she could not see over that lip, but there was a flight of stairs carved into the rock that led up to it. She could also see that mist was flowing off the lip like a waterfall. Kate shivered, knowing that the source of the mistflow must be their destination.

Coming around to the base of the stairs, Kate paused before she followed the Purp-Eyed leader. Hundreds of steps with identical worn dips from countless pilgrimages led straight up to the top.

And at the top? Kate saw a mammoth bolder of turquoise, purples, golds and indigos, all glowing with an iridescent beauty. Her mouth formed an "O." Aside from the eyes of the Purps, this was the only color Kate had seen since she had stepped into the Place-Between-Worlds. It was beautiful, a balm for her color-starved eyes, and she soaked it up eagerly. Then she began to climb, her feet fitting easily into the shallow grooves created by hundreds of footfalls that had gone before her, never taking her eyes from the beautiful boulder.

Only it wasn't a boulder. As she drew closer, the boulder shifted and she saw that it was alive. Her eyes widened as fear lanced into her belly. The bitter taste of bile was in her mouth as the monster rose from its seat, higher and higher, and its wings unfurled, stretched wide in an unimaginable span of shimmering, leather-like skin. Mist was pouring from its nostrils as its neck stretched gracefully, lifting its face to the sky, and then swinging around, its golden eyes fastening onto Kate with keen intelligence.

If her mouth hadn't been so dry, Kate would have screamed. She shook her head, unable to comprehend what she was seeing. *This can't be! Dragons are fables, aren't they? They are myths, aren't they? They can't be real, can they?*

It was all finally too much for Kate. Her eyes rolled up into her head and she surrendered to oblivion.

The lead Purp grabbed Kate by her backpack as she crumpled. He gently carried her the rest of the way up the stairway.

From her loosened grip, TinneHolm floated to its maker.

* * *

Kate regained consciousness in the middle of a conversation. She lay where she was with her eyes closed, listening. The peculiar thing was the conversation seemed to be flowing back and forth through her head, like it was a telephone line.

"…no, Mog, it was nothing you could have foreseen. You have done an excellent job keeping the little Maiden safe. I am proud of you," said one voice.

The other voice, answered in short phrases and words, feelings really. *"Like Maiden. Share food, water. Not hurt?"*

"No, my Battle Hound, she is not hurt." There was a hint of laughter around the edges. *"I believe she was unprepared for me,*

52

the poor child. It must have come as quite a shock. Do not worry, she will soon discover I am not an enemy."

Kate felt warm breath on her face.

"Mog worried. Little Sword Maiden is still asleep."

"Do not worry, Mog. She's awake. She's just gathering information."

Mog licked her face.

Kate scrunched up, trying to escape the slobber. She opened her eyes, her vision filled with Mog's grin.

"Mog." Kate said. "You're name is Mog and you are a Battle Hound."

The Battle Hound's grin widened.

"You see? Little Maiden is keen-witted."

Once more, laughter flowed through Kate's mind like the whisper of dried leaves. *"Yes, she is, but is she brave enough to gaze upon me?"*

Kate swallowed and raised her eyes upwards where, towering above, she was captured within the gaze of the dragon.

"Greetings, Kate, Sword Maiden, Ally of TinneHolm, Eaeda of Ioho, Walker-Between-Worlds, and Bond Mate to Ash of Brendt. I

am called Clarion, last of my Company. Your people know me as the Ancient One. Do not fear, your Sword Ally is safe."

When the dragon had mentioned TinneHolm, Kate's hand had flown to her side. With a sigh, she noticed that her sword was resting between the dragon's powerful forefeet, each claw longer than her blade, and obviously just as sharp.

Kate cleared her throat. "I-I never expected an Ancient One to be a dragon." Her voice sounded tinny to her ears.

The dragon chuckled. *"I gathered that,"* she replied. *"And have you recovered?"*

Kate fingered her braid, raising herself onto her elbows and glancing up at the jowls of Mog, realizing she must have been resting on his feet.

"I can assure you that you are quite safe," the Ancient One told her. *"I did not summon you here to eat you. Why don't you sit up, find a comfortable seating arrangement, so that we may partake of a conversation?"*

Kate did as she was told, and noticed that her backpack had already been removed. She opened it, brought out her water bottle, and took a sip. It helped clear the fog from her mind.

"The mists," Kate said abruptly. "What exactly are they?"

"Very keen-witted, Mog," the dragon thought approvingly.

Mog thumped his tail.

"You have guessed correctly, Kate, that the mists are my creation," Clarion explained. *"I use them to gather information and to conceal my Battle Hounds, keeping them safe. This place was not always as you now see it, Maiden. If you can imagine, I once blended in beautifully with my environment. What you see before you is camouflage from a different Age."*

Kate gasped, trying to imagine what it must have been like when Clarion's exquisite coloration hid her from view. She couldn't.

"It must have been very beautiful," was all she could think to reply.

"Beautiful is just beginning to describe what once was."

"What happened?"

"Greed. Betrayal. War. Death. And stupidity," the Ancient One added after a pause. *"The Company had become too lax. Even with a gift for prophecy, we failed to see the signs. We paid dearly, and now it may be too late to rectify such a dreadful error."*

"How so?"

"Look into my eyes, Young One," the dragon said into Kate's mind.

Kate did so, and found herself falling into deep golden pools of ancient wisdom. Feelings poured into her, engulfing her. Sorrow. Loneliness. Desperation. Weariness. The dragon was at the point

55

of breaking, and she was so very, very tired. Kate felt tears sliding down her face. She felt a need to reach out and to comfort. And then, as if they were never there, the feelings left her.

As Kate came back into herself, one hand was reaching towards the dragon's muzzle.

"*My dear,*" Clarion said. *"Forgive me. I was not aware how open your heart is. I did not mean to burden you with my sorrows. I meant merely to give you a taste so that you would understand the things of which I am about to speak.*"

Silently, Kate wrapped her arms around the magnificent creature's face, stroking its cheek as she would a horse. In fact, the dragon's features reminded Kate of a horse, one covered with beautiful scales. A sea-horse, perhaps.

She waited.

With a sigh, the great bejeweled head leaned into the comfort the young woman offered.

"*It has been a great many years,*" Clarion said. "*I thank you.*"

Kate nodded.

They stood together for a long while.

Mog whined. The other Hounds shifted positions.

Finally, Clarion lifted her head from the girl's shoulder, her head rising high on her slender neck. She shifted her bulk so that she could hunker down like a cat, forelegs tucked neatly beneath her breast, pointed tail curled around. Her neck arched into a graceful "S" curve. The large, iridescent head was now level with Kate's.

"May I tell you a story?"

Looking around, Kate found a rock and sat, elbows on her knees, chin in her hands. "Yes, please."

The Hounds settled in, too.

Chapter 7 - Clarion's Story

"Long ago in the Ancient Times, when the Company was whole, the Place-Between-Worlds was the hub for all the worlds. All pathways still lead to this Place. That is why you Walkers always come to this Place when you are traveling between worlds. Little do you realize that you are traveling upon roads crafted long ago to all the worlds that had been created.

"You see, this Place-Between-Worlds is really the First World, the Company, the First People, although it later was populated by a wide variety of creatures, many you would recognize from your myths and legends"

"Like gryphons, centaurs and mermaids?" Kate asked.

The Ancient One chuckled, mist puffing from her nostrils. *"Since there are dragons, do you not think there would be the others?"*

"Point taken," Kate responded, crossing her legs. "I will do my best not to interrupt again."

Clarion nodded, her voice once more flowing within Kate's mind.

"In addition to the gryphons, centaurs and mermaids, there were also many kinds of people, humans that were more-than-human. These many, varied more-than-humans far outnumbered your gryphons, centaurs and mermaids. Nonetheless, peace reigned within the First World. The Company ruled wisely.

"But there was one group of people who charmed us above all others: the forefathers of your Earth people and of your Bond Mate, those of Ruis. They were a clever and gifted people; beautiful, strong, creative, intelligent. We picked them to guide, shared our wisdom, and, over several hundred years, we allowed them to rule in our stead. We continued to oversee their doings, but not enough. No, not nearly enough."

The dragon paused.

Kate waited.

A Hound shifted its weight.

Another yawned, its great pink tongue curling at the tip, teeth flashing white against its black lips.

With a great sigh that sounded like a giant bellows, Clarion continued.

"Several more centuries came and went.

"All the while the Searn, as your forefathers called themselves, were using the roadways between worlds to expand. With the advanced knowledge that we had gifted them, they built an empire. They mirrored what we had taught, passing on our knowledge to a selected few on each world.

"Several more centuries passed, and the Searn did what the Company did—they allowed the other worlds to rule in their stead,

continuing to oversee their doings, but not enough. Not nearly enough.

"How the desire to expand and enlighten changed into the desire to conquer and enslave, we do not know. Perhaps it is a design flaw within the fundamental composition of the Searn. It is something that was not a part of the Company, and since it is not known to us, it was not seen by us. Neither did we comprehend the warnings in our prophesies.

"That was our fatal flaw.

"For you see, a fraction of the Searn created a new hub for their empire, created new pathways and portals. And then they attacked the First World, took our source of power—the Company's Immortality—and left the First World as you see it today.

"We did what we could, breathing our fire to hold back the enemy, keeping our portals open so that others could escape. We found the portals the Searn had used to attack and managed to close them as well."

The Ancient One paused momentarily before continuing.

"And then we did a terrible thing.

"We brought an unnatural death upon this land so that the remaining Searn army would die."

Clarion shuddered and paused again. Misery seeped through the mental link. If it would have helped, Kate would have hugged the sorrowful creature again. But she knew it wouldn't, thinking it better to let the story continue, so she waited quietly.

In time, Clarion continued.

"We did what we could to protect what little knowledge was left. For each of the new worlds of the displaced peoples, we wrote holy books filled with wisdom and prophesies to guard against anything so terrible happening again. We blocked the pathways created by the Searn, so that their self-created hub was kept from further expansion. And we created the Battle Hounds to guard and protect our First World. We also created other creatures to guard against those portals created by the Searn.

"But we did this at a great cost. Instead of rescuing that which was taken from us—our power, our source of immortality—we sealed it away when we sealed away the Searn. We did this because we did not want to risk our own capture or, worse, their discovering the one last portal that we kept open. We could not bring ourselves to damn a whole civilization because of an error we ourselves had created.

"For, you see, that one portal was a tiny link between the Searn and the First World. If the Searn were completely separated from the First World, they truly would become damned, set adrift from the Whole for Eternity. Most likely they would perish, their life

forces swallowed up into nothingness. But as a link, they could still endanger the First World and First People.

"And so, the final choice had to be made.

"The Company's lifespan is naturally a long one, but without our power, we became finite beings. Our seers foresaw as far as they could. They saw a time where a shift would come, but it was so far into the future they doubted that we would be alive to take advantage of the shift and heal our mistakes. So we devised a plan. There would be a vote, one of the Company would be chosen. The rest would then gift their remaining life spans to the One, thus ensuring that One would still remain when the foretold shift came to be.

"I was the one selected. I took it as an honor. But now I see it as a curse."

Clarion sighed.

"I am so very old. I am now dying. When I am gone, there will be none to protect the First World. There will be none to guard the final portal. The Searn believed that if they claimed our Power Source, then their world would replace the First World. This is not the case, and they would not listen to us when we tried to forward this knowing to them.

"The First World is the First World

"If I die, it dies. If it dies, all worlds will die."

Chapter 8 - The Quest

Kate gasped.

"I see that you understand my dilemma. Even with the life spans that were gifted to me, the time is not yet ready, and I will not survive to see it through. I will die and, with my death, all life."

"Even the Power Source that was stolen?"

The Ancient One nodded her great head. *"Even that. I can feel it weakening."* She chuckled without humor. *"There was a time when we argued what came first, ourselves or our source of power. I appear to have stumbled upon the answer."*

"So you need to get it back," Kate stated.

The dragon chuckled again. *"Ever the clever one, this Sword Maiden, is that not so, Mog?"*

The Battle Hound thumped his tail and grinned at Kate before he yawned and stretched out at the lip of the cave.

"And how do you think that will come to be?"

"Isn't that why you summoned my sword? To summon me?" Kate asked.

"I summoned your sword to summon you to summon your Bond Mate."

Kate scowled. "Ash? Why?"

"Because he Walked through stone".

Kate was silent, then shuddered. "I was thinking about that day while the Purps...um Battle Hounds...and I were crossing that plateau and passed the spot where Ash brought us out. We nearly didn't make it. If Joey hadn't been hanging on to some redwood needles, we would most likely have been eaten by a giant Scorpion Thing."

"Joey, is he the one called Ioho?"

Kate nodded. "He's the Chosen One and, since you are an Ancient One, he's the one you prophesied about."

Clarion dipped her head at Kate. *"So it would seem. He is a wise child. He thinks like one of the Company, like the First People."*

"He is wise..." Kate agreed. Her voice trailed off.

"And this troubles you?"

Kate chuckled. "No, it's just that nobody allows him to simply be a kid, you know? For all that he is, he still deserves some sort of childhood."

"You do the allowing, Maiden. He is fortunate to have you."

"Thank you," Kate said. "I really think I needed to hear that. So...thanks."

"You will remain his touchstone to his humanness, I believe."

Kate sipped again from her water. "So, do we just sit and wait for Ash to find me?" she asked.

"All Bonded pairs can connect with one another. We shall wait."

"Would you like me to try to connect with Ash?"

"Since your mate is not with you, I have assumed there is an important reason for this. We will wait until that reason is completed."

Kate considered what the Ancient One said. Finding a safer haven for Joey and their Kinsmen was very important, and their Kinsmen needed Ash for that. If the dragon said they could wait, then they could.

"Do you even know where your Power Source is?"

"I do. One has to move through the remaining portal to reclaim it. A portal of stone."

Kate folded her hands and rested her chin on them. "Suppose," she began, "you had something that was like your Power Source. I could link with that, and go get it myself. I'm a Walker, after all. Joey handed Ash the redwood needles that were from the Grandfathers, and that's how Ash tracked them. I could do the same, if you had something like that. I'd go, grab your Power

Source, and back I'd come. Easy," Kate said, miming her actions with her hands.

The dragon unfurled her ruff as she swung her head around to eye Kate more closely. *"An interesting concept, Maiden. Let me ponder this."*

Clarion curled her head around her body as if she were sleeping, while Kate looked on. The dragon was still for so long that Kate thought perhaps the Ancient One had simply dozed off, like old people are known to do. Kate stretched and glanced over at Mog. Like the rest of the Purps, he was sprawled on his side with eyes closed and paws twitching. *Nap time,* Kate thought. She grinned.

Much later, with a scaly rustle, the dragon lifted her head. Kate, who had been studying the landscape, trying again to imagine it beautiful and green, refocused upon Clarion.

"I have devised a plan, Maiden, and am rather pleased with it. I can give you what you need, and I believe I can help ease you through the rock. Rest yourself while I prepare." The dragon studied her. *"I am in a desperate situation. I do so hope that this desperation is not overriding my judgment. The place where I am sending you, Maiden, is not for the faint of heart, nor is there a guarantee you will return."*

A shiver ran through Kate. She swallowed hard. "If nothing is done, then we all die. If I don't make it, then there is Ash."

The dragon studied her for what seemed to Kate a very long time. The deep golden gaze seemed to look into the very heart of her. She felt pinned by that gaze; there was no way she could even blink. Finally the dragon released her. Kate slumped back.

"TinneHolm has chosen wisely, very wisely indeed. Go now, and rest by Mog. My Hound will protect you. I need to keep the sword for a little while."

Upon hearing his name, Mog opened one eye and thumped his tail.

Kate watched the massive dragon heave herself to her feet, noticing how tired the creature seemed. Clarion turned gracefully and disappeared into the cave, TinneHolm floating beside her. Kate got onto her knees and crawled over to the leader of the Purps. Using her backpack as a pillow, she lay down beside him.

She wondered if she was being too impetuous. Should she have waited for Ash? She thought about how long it had taken to get to Clarion's cave. She thought of the giant scorpion things and the huge wasteland that had to be crossed. Without the Purp-Eyes, it would take Ash a long time to get here, with lots more danger. She wondered if she should try to contact Ash through the Bond Mate connection, to let him know she was okay—scared, but okay. She wondered how the connection worked, or if it would, since they were so newly Bonded. The Ancient One said she had a plan. Kate decided to wait and learn what it was.

With a sigh, she snuggled closer to Mog, grinning to herself because she was lying next to a huge mad scientist experiment. *The things we can adjust to*, she thought. Thinking of Ash, Kate drifted off to sleep.

* * *

Ash and Lorcan stood looking down into a wide valley deep within the mountains of Ruis.

"Now, this is a surprise," the Captain of the Guard murmured. "I wonder why none have found this place before." His eyes scanned the valley floor, imagining the necessary fortification. "If we settled over there," he said, pointing to the far side of the valley where it butted up against cliffs, "our lookouts could give us plenty of time to prepare for defense."

"If we were discovered," commented Ash.

"Aye, if that," Lorcan answered. "We are far from charted territories, to be sure." He studied the landscape further. "I like this place," he said abruptly. "I think we should go back to the encampment, collect a few scouts, bring them back, turn 'em lose, and then continue on our hunt."

"My only concern is the need to be prepared for the winter months," Ash said, "when game gets scarce. Over the past two years, I have been asked to fetch more and more supplies."

"A concern, to be sure," Lorcan agreed. "But we have some good hunters amongst us. Does not Declan have the Hunter's Gift?"

"Aye, I forgot about Declan," Ash agreed.

Ash took great care masking their trail as they returned to the Brendt encampment. As the Lady Faith had pointed out, Ruis was large, but not that large. The more they moved, the fewer places would be left to move to. The three places that he and Lorcan were scouting to find would need to be safe for a good many years. That need for safety was forcing Brendt into isolation, a situation that would make them totally dependent upon their Walkers. He made a mental note to show Kate how to better mask their trail. She needed work in that one area.

Kate! He felt a smile begin as he wondered how she was doing with her mission. Had TinneHolm found the Ancient One? What was to be asked of the sword and its Maiden? Ash was torn between wanting to be with his Bond Mate and doing what he could to help his Kinsmen. Had she not been the warrior he knew her to be, he would never have left her side.

Ash brought Lorcan through a portal close to the Brendt. They emerged into the sounds of a camp in the midst of being torn down and packed away. Tents were partially dismantled. Furnishings were packed and stacked in rows and in the process of being labeled and catalogued before being placed in wagons. Looking at the mounds of belongings, Ash realized that it was up to Kate and him to Walk their Kinsmen and all their belongings to the new encampments. He felt tired just looking at it all. When had the Brendt become such packrats, he wondered?

"Such a difference from where we just were, eh?" commented Lorcan. "I'm going to round up some scouts and meet with you at half past." He cast a sidelong glance at Ash as he studied the mountain of possessions.

"Looks rather daunting, lad."

Ash smiled grimly and nodded. "It will have to be done in stages, that it will," he replied. "A Walker can only bring so much through at a time."

Lorcan clapped a hand on Ash's shoulder. "If ever it can be done, it can be done by you and your Bond Mate. I've great faith in the two of you."

"We will do what needs to be done," Ash assured him.

Lorcan went to select his scouts while Ash headed for what used to be the cooking tent for some supplies. On his way, be bumped into Faith, who looked at him in surprise.

"Ash!" she said, sweeping her silvery hair from her eyes, "Here again! So soon?"

"Aye," Ash replied with a smile. He always enjoyed moments with Faith. "Lorcan's getting some scouts so we can turn them loose at what looks to be a fine, fair place, a pristine valley."

Faith's eyes lighted up, "That's good news, Ash The sooner the task is completed, the sooner you'll be back with your Kate," she said with a nudge. "It's hardly been a day, but I wager you're missing your Mate."

Ash thought he was beyond blushing, but Faith managed to pull one out of him. "I miss her indeed, that I do," he said softly.

"Well, I wouldn't worry about her," Faith said, touching his arm. "She's a Sword Maiden with one of the best sword allies in TinneHolm."

"Aye, I know the sword well."

"That's right! TinneHolm was your mother's before," Faith replied.

"That it was. Now, if you'll excuse me, Lorcan wants to hurry," Ash said politely, hoping he would have a chance to check on Ioho before he needed to leave.

"And I certainly don't need to be gathering moss with you, my boy!" said Faith with a laugh. "Good hunting!"

"Thank you, good packing to you."

Faith's laugh tinkled in her wake as she hurried on .

Ash smiled, watching her go, then turned in search for food and Ioho.

He found the boy playing with two other youngsters and a child guardian, out of the traffic. Before Ash could speak, the boy's head whipped around, and he was up and running towards him.

Ash laughed as Ioho's arms bear-hugged his legs.

"I am happy to see you, too, that I am," he said, scooping the boy up and returning the hug.

He put his forehead to the boy's, while the tot's small hands patted the sides of his face. "I'm finding fine new homes for us, Ioho. Two more to go."

"Kate?" Joey asked, drawing back to look in Ash's eyes.

"Ah, she is still on her own mission, but I expect we will all be together soon."

Joey patted Ash's cheek. "Be ready," he said seriously. Then he smiled and handed Ash the three-inch piece of rock he was carrying. "Pretty. For luck."

Ash glanced at it and then took a closer look. It wasn't just an ordinary pebble the boy had handed him. It was milky-pink and translucent, warm to the touch. "Where did you discover this treasure?" he asked the boy as he tucked it into his shirt pocket.

Joey shrugged. "Good for boo-boos," he said, squirming to get down.

Ash smiled at the term borrowed from Kate and set the boy on his feet. The moment his feet touched the ground, he dashed back to his playmates. "You stay out of harm's way, now, Ioho. I will come check on you next time I return," he called after Joey, who was already fixated on returning to his play. Ash laughed and nodded cordially to the child guardian.

With his pack replenished with food and drink, Ash went back to the ever-growing pile of belongings that he and Kate would be Walking. He stood shaking his head, waiting for Lorcan, wondering if they realized what an effort this move would be for their Walkers. He wished that he and Kate were free to enjoy themselves, have a proper honeymoon, as she had called it.

"That pile of junk still's got ye worried, eh?" asked Lorcan as he approached with four scouts.

"It is daunting, to be sure." Ash said.

"Perhaps some could be brought overland."

"We would be risking discovery." Ash replied.

"Something to discuss with the Council, then," Lorcan replied calmly. "Well I've managed to round up these lads, and we're outfitted and ready to go when you are," Lorcan added, changing the subject.

Ash surveyed the men, "Who's Walked before?" he asked.

They all had, save Declan, the Hunter, a large, freckled man with long ginger hair. "I prefer my own two feet," he told Ash, rather nervously.

Ash smiled. "Just close your eyes and you'll be fine."

He positioned the men in a line, putting Declan first. "Hold on, one to the other. Keep moving once we start," Ash told them. "Remember, do *not* let go, or you break the energy chain."

Since all but Declan knew what to expect, the walk through the two portals was swift and easy. As they arrived at the valley, Declan abruptly sat down, causing the others to stumble and leap aside to avoid him.

Declan put a hand to either side of his head. *"By the gods!"* he exclaimed, freckles standing out starkly against the whiteness of his face. "I do believe that I still prefer my own two feet." He glanced up at Ash. "No offense."

Ash grinned. "None taken. It is a thing that one needs to settle into."

"I will not argue with ye on that matter," Declan answered with sharp laugh. "Tis a thing I hope to avoid settling into," he added, as he stood and brushed off his leather pants.

"That decides it, then," said Lorcan, catching the end of the conversation. "Declan, you and Logan here, scout out this valley. Ye've two days until we come back to collect ya. Be here at this spot."

"Two days' time. We'll take our leave, then," Declan replied.

Ash watched the two scouts settle into a ground-eating walk, heads together, and pointing out various landmarks as they disappeared into the valley. He turned to the three remaining men. "Ready?"

"Aye," replied Lorcan. "I've an eye set towards that far ridge," he said nodding at a line of mountains on the other side of the valley where they were standing. "I want us to be difficult for the Lophft to find. However, if our Kinsmen will be going back and forth among the three encampments, they should all be within a day's pace. I'm thinking signal fires on the ridges in between could prove a good early warning system."

The other two scouts, Tate and Liam by name, nodded in agreement.

"Then to that ridge we will go," replied Ash. He centered himself to sense a trail and vision a portal opening into the far ridge. When it had become clear in his mind, he reached out a hand that was gripped by Lorcan. "Ready?"

"Aye," the three men answered in unison.

Ash Walked and led them through to the ridge. The valley on the other side was just as empty and verdant as the one they had just left. From where they stood, they could see into both.

Lorcan clasped his hands together with a loud clap. "Excellent place for a lookout site. Well pleased I am!" he said, slowly turning and scanning the horizons. His eyebrows shot up, "Fellas, look there! Do ye see where these two valleys meet in a V? If we placed our third encampment there, from where we stand, we could see all three." His eyes sparkled with excitement. "I do believe tha—"

The wave of pain that shot through Ash was so sudden and so intense that he could not stifle his cry. His knees buckled. The edges of his vision darkened. Another wave of pain swept through his body, sharp and jagged. He gasped and would have fallen into a fetal position if not for Lorcan's strong arms holding him still.

"Ash! Can ye hear me, lad?" Lorcan said as if from a long distance.

Kate! The pain was Kate's!

"Kate! I need to go. Now." He hauled himself to his feet and pulled free from Lorcan's steadying grasp.

"Aye, Lad. I see that ye must."

Without a backward glance, Ash raced to the nearest tree and opened a portal. But he did not come out in the Place-Between-Worlds. Instead, he was pulled in some other direction. *How can this be?* Never had he Walked without a pause Between-Worlds. Fear laced through him, but his driving need to reach Kate overcame his fear, and he pressed on, clinging to the link of a Bonded Pair like a lifeline. It felt as if he were Walking through thick mud. His lungs were full of the thick energy and he feared he would suffocate. Sweat beaded up on his forehead. His ears rang. Once again the edges of his vision began to darken, but he banked the rising fear and focused all the more on Kate.

He still felt her pain. His fear shifted into a fear for his Bond Mate.

Something was very, very wrong.

He made one final effort to push through. To Kate.

Chapter 9 - The Searn

Kate woke when Mog moved the furry paw that she had been using as a pillow.

"Ow!" she said, rubbing her cheek and scowling at the Battle Hound, wondering why she had been on his paw in the first place. She must have chosen it over her backpack while she was asleep, she decided. Expecting the usual grin, she was surprised to see that he looked rather contrite.

She froze to attention when she heard the rustling dry leaves sound that meant Clarion was coming. Butterflies played havoc in Kate's stomach. Soon she would know Clarion's plan, and her quest would begin. Rubbing the sleep from her eyes, she sat up, facing the cave mouth and wishing for a facecloth. While stifling a yawn, she waited for the Ancient One to emerge.

Mog *woofed* and the pack came to attention, standing in a semicircle around the opening behind Mog and Kate.

TinneHolm floated out through wisps of mist and settled into Kate's hands. Behind the sword came the dragon, immense and lovely, scales flashing blues, greens, golds and purples. Kate paused and reveled in Clarion's magnificence, her mouth curving into a half smile. Mog gently tugged on Kate's jerkin, ensuring that she was out of the way when the huge tail came sweeping past.

The dragon's golden eyes landed upon the group, and she accepted their respectful demeanors.

"And are you rested?" Her thoughts rustled through their minds. *"Are you ready to execute my plan?"*

Kate sensed the dragon's excitement and her hope, her heart responding in kind.

"I'm ready." Her stomach growled loudly. Kate clamped a hand over it. "Sorry," she said, feeling her cheeks grow pink.

Mog swung his huge head at Kate, small ears pricking forward, and grinned.

"Do you have nourishment with which to break your fast? You will need your strength," Clarion asked.

Kate nodded.

"Then, please, eat. I shall tell you my plan as you do so."

"Thanks," Kate replied. She leaned TinneHolm gently against a rock and sat next to her Sword Ally. Reaching over, she snagged her backpack and found the stash of dried meat and fruit she had brought with her.

She began eating, but paused when she noticed how the Battle Hounds watched her, their heads rising and falling in unison as they tracked her hand as it went back and forth from food to mouth. She couldn't help laughing, and cheerfully threw a bit of meat to each.

The dragon watched with amusement and growing affection before explaining her plan.

"I was present at the birth of TinneHolm. It was our dragon fire in which the twenty-one swords were forged. It was with dragon magic that they were ensouled and animated. Therefore, TinneHolm and I can communicate was well as the sword communicates with you, its Ally. This being so, TinneHolm knows exactly how to maneuver through the stone portal to the world of the Searn. The sword will guide you on your Walk."

The dragon paused and waited for Kate to nod with understanding before she continued.

"Now this—" the dragon paused again and opened up her great clawed forefoot, turning it upwards. In the center was a large disc, slightly oval and slightly curving, about four feet tall and three feet wide. Kate's first impression was of a giant contact lens. It would have fit perfectly over Clarion's eye.

She giggled, then clamped a hand over her mouth, mortified.

Clarion looked at her sharply, frills raised in indignation.

"I-I am so sorry, Ancient One," Kate exclaimed. "I don't know what came over me. It must be nerves."

"Understood," came the reply. The frill laid flat again.

Kate refocused on the object.

"This will lead you to my Power Source.   It is the same substance."

Setting her pack and food down, Kate stood and crossed over to the dragon's forefoot that held the offering. Her eyes widened.

"A shield?"

"That is correct. A shield fashioned from one of my own scales. Take it. Use caution. Except where it was detached from my body, the edges are as sharp as Tinneholm's blade."

 Kate looked wonderingly at the dragon and then reached forward to grasp the dragon scale shield by the two handles that were somehow attached to its inside.

"Dragon magic," Clarion explained.

As she lifted it, Kate staggered backwards, not because it was heavy, but because its lightness had caught her off guard.

The outside of the shield gave off the same iridescent sheen as Clarion.   "It's beautiful," Kate breathed, watching the greens, blues, purples and golds playing across its surface. "So very beautiful." She glanced back up at the dragon, its lovely head towering far above Kate. "And this will take me to your Power Source?" she asked.

"That it shall do. The Power Source and I are One."

Kate squinted up at the Ancient One. "And what exactly does this Power Source look like?"

"My Power Source is an egg."

Kate cocked her head. "Excuse me?"

"An egg. It is how we remain immortal. When our bodies become too burdensome, then our essence is transferred into the new life that is contained within the egg. We die and are born again."

"Oh! Like a Phoenix."

"Exactly so. Phoenixes are a distant relative. However, there are many differences. My egg is my Power Source. My egg is the source of my life and also the source of my magic, possibly of all magic. We were the first beings. Life flowed through us to all other beings."

Kate nodded, reflectively. "Okay. Let me make sure I've got this right. TinneHolm leads me to where the Searn live. The shield leads me to where your egg is. I get the egg and bring it back to you. I'm assuming that I will be led back to you, because I will have both your egg and your scale."

"The return should be much easier. My Power Source and I yearn for one another. It should easily bring you back."

Kate nodded again. Then she put her arm through the shield. It covered a good portion of her body. "All the vulnerable places," she murmured to herself. She discovered that if she slid it high enough on to her arm, one strap was fastened around her upper arm and the other was about her lower, leaving both her hands free to wield TinneHolm. "Excellent!" she declared, as she removed the new shield. She looked up at the dragon. "Thank you, Ancient One. I am honored to have this gift."

"I am honored that you accept it. Please also accept Mog, my Battle Hound. Take him with you."

Kate's eyes widened and she looked at Mog, who grinned and thumped his tail. She grinned back at him. "I am doubly honored." she said, reaching down for TinneHolm. She strapped the sword back at her side where it belonged. After putting on her pack and cinching down the straps, Kate slipped the shield in place. "I am ready, Ancient One," she announced.

"Come, then," Clarion replied, turning back into the cave, trailing the telltale mists in her wake.

Leaving the Battle Hound pack to guard the cave mouth, Kate and Mog followed the dragon down into a wide tunnel that looked exactly like a lava tube. And perhaps, Kate mused as she skillfully dodged Clarion's tail, it was created just like a lava tube, only the rock-melting heat would have been supplied by dragons, not a volcano.

She thought it would be darker, but that same translucent light came softly from the tube's walls. As they headed deeper into the mountain, the tube began to level out. At the bottom, it expanded into an enormous cavern, large enough, Kate imagined, to hold several dragons. Stalactites hung like frozen icicles, glistening far above Kate's head. The dry walls seemed moist as they glistened and sparkled. "Now this is exactly how I imagined a dragon's lair to be like!" Kate said to Mog, who merely grinned.

In the center of the cavern was a circle of twelve pillars that towered several inches above Kate's head. It was to this circle of pillars that Clarion walked. When she arrived, she turned to the young woman and the Battle Hound.

"This is our nest. We kept our eggs on the top of each of these columns, one column for each of the Company. And in the center of these columns is the final portal into Searn that I guard. As I have stated, the Searn believe that this portal is also closed.

"When I activate it, they will realize that it has not been destroyed. You will not have much time before they detect your presence in their kingdom. When they find you, they will either destroy you or follow you, should you escape. I have decided that this portal is too dangerous, whether or not you are successful. I will keep it open for a span of time.

"After that span of time, I will destroy it. If you have not returned, you and my Battle Hound will remain in Searn. I tell you this, Maiden, so that you have all the facts. I would not hold it against you should you decide that this is too dangerous a quest for you to attempt."

"But I am a Walker," Kate argued, "Why can't I just open up a portal if this one is closed? I will still have the shield and the egg to help me lock onto you."

"When I am no longer alive and dragon magic is gone from all worlds, perhaps you could. But not until then, Maiden. Even then it is uncertain. It would be as if the tunnel from the cave mouth to my nest had collapsed."

"Then how could Ash open the portal on the plateau?"

"Although closed to the Searn world, there was always the possibility that it could be used as a pathway for a Walker. What you must understand, Maiden, is that once the portal before you is destroyed, there will be no more portals open between the Searn world and all other worlds."

Kate nodded and took a deep breath to calm her pounding heart. "Well, okay, then," she said after a time. "How much time do I have?"

"Once the portal is open, you will have a span of one hour."

Kate gasped and gripped her sword more tightly.

85

"You will know when the time is ending, as the portal will weaken and flicker. This portal is unlike those created by Walkers. It remains open unless deliberately closed. Again, think of a tunnel that will collapse. It will begin to collapse from the Searn's opening to this opening. This is why it is so dangerous. When you see the flickering, it will signify that the portal is beginning to collapse from your direction. Do you understand the possible consequences of your choice?"

Kate thought of Ash and of Joey. She thought of the aging dragon and the end of the First World, followed by all worlds.

She nodded. "Yes, Ancient One, I understand the consequences of my choice. I will go to Searn, and I will bring you back your egg."

"Are you ready?"

Kate swallowed. "Yes, Ancient One, I am ready."

"Very well. I shall now open the portal."

The dragon opened her mouth, and a steady stream of mist swirled out in a corkscrew spiral. The mist congealed and hardened into a doorway that shimmered with a thin membrane.

"Looks like a soap bubble before someone blows on it," commented Kate.

"The portal is open, Maiden. You have the span of one hour, and then it will be destroyed."

Kate swallowed and took a deep breath, imagining a soap bubble popping and disappearing. She pulled TinneHolm from its scabbard. Noticing how it glowed once more, she held it forward, with one hand. With her other hand she adjusted her shield so the edges wouldn't cut Mog. Then she grabbed a fistful of the Battle Hound's fur. Together, they stepped through the membrane.

* * *

Walking the Searn's pathway through rock was not like anything Kate could have imagined. She had braced herself for an experience similar to when Ash had taken them through the stone fireplace at her home. This felt much the same, thick and viscous and nearly impassable.

But it seemed to take forever to push through the thick tar-like substance in which they were Walking. She kept waiting for the inevitable pause and rest at the Place-Between-Worlds. If she hadn't had such a sinking feeling when she remembered that they had begun their Walk from The Place-Between-Worlds, she would have laughed.

As more time passed in the thick atmosphere, she became clammy with sweat, and her lungs begged for relief. Kate thought she heard Mog whine, but couldn't be sure. When they finally burst through, Kate sank to one knee, gasping for breath. She waited before she released her grip on Mog, grateful for his big strong shoulder. He licked her face.

"Earlier, I wished for a facecloth," she groused affectionately to the Hound. "Now I need a towel."

Kate let go of him and stood, moving a little away from the Purp to keep a safe, sword-width distance between them. Her eyes widened as she scanned her surroundings. "Would you look at that!" she whispered, slowly turning around.

They had just Walked into an exact replica of Clarion's cave, but it was smaller, and there was an egg on each of the twelve pedestals.

As with the other cave, there was only one opening, with lots of space for sword swinging, but little cover except for the columns.

"Guard the door, Mog," she told the Battle Hound. "In and out we go," she muttered.

Mog crossed over to the small opening, and Kate went to the columns, that were, like the ones in Clarion's cave, taller than she was. Placing TinneHolm within easy reach, Kate removed her shield and backpack and stood, hands on her hips, trying to figure out a way to get Clarion's egg, which was easy to pick out, as it was glowing strongly in the same colors as the shield. She crossed over to the column and tipped her head back, feeling for finger holds. It was as smooth as glass. Annoyed that she hadn't asked Clarion how fragile a dragon egg was, she looked at a neighboring egg and decided, since Clarion said it was dead, that she would experiment on it.

With the tip of her sword, she gently prodded the egg until it began to wobble. Then with a flick, she unseated it, catching it as she would a football. She studied it as it lay cradled in the crook of her arm. Close up, Kate saw that the egg was actually about the size a football, perhaps a little smaller, and was, well, egg-shaped. Its exterior was leathery and much less fragile than Kate had thought. And the color! It was beautiful. This one was a swirl of reds and golds and yellows. The more she stared at it, the more the colors seemed to swirl and dance. Kate closed her eyes, envisioning how beautiful the dragon must have been. How sad to think it was gone forever, having given the last of its life to keep Clarion alive.

Suddenly Kate realized she did not have the heart to leave the egg in Searn. She had to bring it back. It deserved a burial or something. They all did, she decided, glancing around at the rest.

Still holding the red egg, Kate went over to her backpack and emptied its contents. She set the egg down on her pile of spare clothes and peered into the now-empty pack. Could it hold twelve eggs, she wondered? With all the outside pockets that Kate was busily emptying, she thought perhaps it could. It must!

With TinneHolm's help, Kate easily dislodged and caught the other eggs, one at a time, laying them in her clothes nest until she had all twelve in a gorgeous, glowing pile. She squatted beside them and reached for the backpack.

She paused in mid-reach.

The dragon eggs were glowing!

What was happening?

At that moment Mog whined, then growled deep in his throat, his thick, fluffy fur making a ridge all the way down his back.

As fast as she could, Kate began to pack up the eggs, filling the pockets first. Clarion's egg was the first to go into the center, and she gently placed the others on top of it as quickly as she could. With one last egg to go, Kate was relieved to see she was somehow managing to make them all fit.

She smelled the Searn even before she heard them.

They *reeked*! They smelled like death and decay.

Nauseating.

She heard them next, a tramping of marching feet growing louder and louder, the sound echoing off the cavern's walls.

And then she saw them. A horde of them. They filled up the lava tube, nearly blocking all the light that had filtered in from the opening. They would have kept coming if Mog had not stood in their path, eyes flaring, fangs bared, sounding his deep, earth-vibrating growl.

Kate stood slowly, egg in hand, mouth agape. *What were these creatures?* They looked like husks, sour things eaten up from the inside out. Evil things, with calculating and greedy glances. She was not even able to call them human-like. Is this what happens when all you focus on is power, Kate wondered? Was there anything redeeming about them? She thought not.

"Put down that Power Source," the Searn in front said as he pointed a laser-like rod at her. The other Searn pressed behind him, causing him to stumble.

Kate did as she was told, gently sliding the egg into her backpack with the others, then fastening it up tight. Slowly, she set the pack down behind the shield Clarion had given her, trusting it would protect them.

"That was not my intention, Maiden," the husk snapped in a voice that sounded like fingers on a chalkboard.

Mog's answering growl rumbled in fierce warning.

She had thought to have more time to negotiate, so the Searn caught her off guard when he fired his wand.

But TinneHolm was there. The sword flew into her hands to deflect the thin, greenish-yellow stream of energy. With relief, Kate watched the energy shoot back towards its source. The Searn sizzled. Where it once stood were only fine particles of dust fluttering to the floor. The air smelled sulfuric, and even more of death.

In the slight pause, TinneHolm broke in two.

"Nooooo!" The scream ripped from Kate's throat, followed by a rage and sorrow so huge she could not contain it. As she stared at the two pieces, pain lanced deep into her core, piercing through her body with an agony of loss, and wringing her stomach, twisting it until she retched.

Mog attacked the Searn then, his huge jaws opening wide, unhinging to consume whatever was in his way. He ripped, tore, shredded and swallowed, fathoms-deep growls merging with the screams of pain.

But more kept coming through the open doorway, pushing through by their sheer force of numbers, the living crawling over the bits and pieces of the dead.

They all carried the laser rods.

Mog's yelp of surprise and pain galvanized Kate into action.

She was without her Ally, but she could still fight.

Grabbing the dragon scale, she reached Mog's side in two swift strides. Kate used the scale as both shield and weapon, hacking at the nearest Searn with the shield's sharp edge, hacking and feinting and raging forward like a wild thing, without thought or planning, only knowing that she intended to kill every last one of them as payment for what they had done to her Sword Ally.

Shoulder to shoulder the Sword Maiden and the Battle Hound fought, using the pillars as cover when they were forced back by the throng. For as long as they lasted, the pillars worked. But the endless laser blasts cut them down in no time.

The Searn kept coming, more and more, pushing forward in an endless stream of evil intent upon destruction. The two slew countless Searn, yet their enemy continued to swarm through the opening like angry wasps, and just as deadly. Kate caught the purple-eyed glance of Mog, knowing instinctively what he was communicating to her.

It wasn't hard to see that they could not withstand the onslaught much longer. Despite his great strength and endurance, Mog was weakening. Something was happening to him each time he was shot with a laser. His muzzle and ears were blackening, the tips of his claws. His teeth. She failed to notice that the same thing was happening to her hands, the hands that had held TinneHolm when it had died.

Seeing the spreading black, Kate's heart ached for the noble Hound. One ally had already died.

One was enough.

I have to get us out of here!

She glanced at the portal behind them, horrified to see it flickering and growing dim. It was only going to remain open a little longer. "Mog!" she shouted above the din. "Let's go home!"

Staying behind the shield, she reached her backpack and gently collected the precious cargo. She picked up the pieces that were once her sword and slid them into the pack as well.

Mog's warning bark barely came in time. Kate whirled upon the Searn that had managed to sneak around her, noticing that more were following it.

She leapt at her attacker, blocking the rod that was aimed at her head. It fired, the yellow-green energy barely grazing her shoulder. A stalactite growing from the ceiling exploded. Stone rained down upon them, temporarily blinding the closest Searn. Kate wrenched the laser rod free from the Searn's grasp, aimed, and fired it without a thought. The Searn disappeared in a haze of green stench.

"Mog! Let's go!" she shouted again. The Hound bounded toward her as she gathered up the shield on one arm and her pack in the other. Together, they backed toward the portal opening under a volley of laser fire that lit up the room in a dull yellow fireworks display. Firing in return, Kate tried to keep the shield up to protect both of them as they moved.

When the dizziness stuck, followed by an intense, searing pain, Kate staggered and nearly fell. "What's happening?" she said, suddenly groggy. Flashes of light and patches of black raced in front of her eyes. Her ears began to ring. She desperately tried to focus, raising her injured arm toward the portal, summoning it to glow steadily so she could pull them through.

It wasn't going to be enough.

Chapter 10 - Hope and Despair

Sorrow washed over her, bathing her in despair, "I'm so sorry Mog… Ancient One. I—"

A familiar hand fisted into her clothes, pulling her into the portal.

"Mog, too!" she gasped.

Without pausing, Ash grabbed a handful of Mog's fur and dragged them both roughly through to—where? He did not know. He felt the portal closing from behind as he followed an energy signature back to its source, realizing with a start that whatever Kate was carrying in her pack was helping them through. They stumbled into a semicircle of pillars. Kate and the massive furry creature fell prone. Ash crashed to his knees at the feet of a dragon, a beast he was sure could not be real.

Yet there it was.

Clarion closed and destroyed the last remaining portal into Searn, sighing with the effort it had required to keep it open, yet grieving at having sealed a people forever from the First World.

In the quiet, the Ancient One blinked down at what lay between her paws.

What she felt was hope.

What she saw was despair.

Mog lay sprawled where he had fallen, sides heaving, extremities blackened. The Sword Maiden was lying on her belly beside Mog, hand still gripping a weapon unknown to the Ancient One. Her shield was still attached to the other arm. The other Walker was frozen on his knees, uncertainty in his eyes, but no fear. The Maiden moaned, and he glanced quickly at the young woman and then back up at her. Clarion sent thoughts flowing through the group. Tendrils of mist were already gathering information on the welfare of her Battle Hound.

"You may tend to your Bond Mate, Ash of the Brendt, Walker-Between-Worlds."

The Walker spared the dragon only a brief startled glance before he rushed to the Maiden's side.

"She is fortunate to have one such as you as her Bond-Mate, Ash of the Brendt. She surely would have perished had you not come for her."

Focusing on Kate and momentarily ignoring Clarion, Ash gently pried the laser wand from Kate's grasp, gasping at her blackened fingers. Gingerly, he set the wand aside. He slid the shield from her limp arm, and set it by the laser. Disconnecting the straps from the backpack, he removed it, all without disturbing the unconscious woman. Glancing curiously at its bulging contents, he was about to place it beside Kate's things when the dragon stopped him with her thoughts.

"Ash of the Brendt, would you open it for me?"

With a nod, he did what he was told. He gasped in dismay as he pulled out the two pieces that had been Kate's Sword Ally.

"Oh, Kate, I feel your pain with this," he told the still form. But before he could return to Kate, the dragon spoke again.

"Your Bond Mate is unconscious. She will not benefit from your words at this moment. You must help me first."

Anger and fear surged through him. "May I at least make her comfortable?"

Upon the dragon's consent, Ash quickly removed his own pack and pulled out a blanket and a soft leather shirt. He rolled Kate over, pillowed her head with his shirt, arranged her limbs, and covered her with the blanket. Bending down, he kissed her forehead. "I am not far from you Kate, you are not alone," he whispered.

"Thank you," he said to the dragon, and quietly returned to emptying Kate's pack.

Ash reached in and brought out the first egg. It glowed in his hand, purples and yellows swirling on its leather shell. He held it out, transfixed.

The dragon lowered her head and nuzzled it gently.

"I dare not hope. I dare not."

Ash glanced at the golden eye so very close to his own. "You are disbelieving what you are seeing?"

"That is exactly what I am doing. Please, show me the others. Quickly."

Her burgeoning excitement rippled through him.

With the dragon's mind she lifted the egg in his hand from his grasp and laid it gently onto one of the columns, where it rested high above him. Ash produced another egg for the dragon to see. This one blazed red and orange, as if it were filled with fire.

The dragon's delight swept over Ash as that egg was lifted from his hand and placed upon another column.

The next one he pulled out glowed more brightly than the others.

"My Power Source!"

The dragon's huge head swooped down again as she looked at it with first one eye, and then the other. She shivered, frill raised like a fan.

"I can feel its strength! I can feel my power returning to me."

Beside herself with joy, the beast stretched her neck high and unfurled her wings. Mist streamed from the flared nostrils. Clarion roared, flapping her wings and rattling her scales.

Nearly deafened, Ash flinched. If he weren't filled with her joy, he would have cowered in terror.

Instead, he calmly waited for her to relocate her egg to its pedestal so he could pull another from Kate's pack. And then another. Each egg had its own pattern of swirling colors. Each was incredibly beautiful.

So it went until all twelve eggs were back on their pedestals.

"A miracle! A miracle! The blessed Maiden succeeded when I doubted her! She said she would and she did! Remarkable. A remarkable thing. A miracle".

Ash ignored the dragon. Freed from his duty, he reached for Kate and gathered her unconscious form into his arms. "Oh Kate," he whispered, brushing her red-gold hair from her forehead. "You risk so much. You must come back to me. I need you." He gathered her to his heart, rocking her gently as Clarion watched them.

"The sword and the Hound, I can heal. But with this one, I am unsure. However, I promise you, Ash of the Brendt, I will do all that I can. As you have said, she has risked much. She does not deserve a reward such as this."

* * *

As if from a long distance, Kate heard her name called. Warm and free from pain, she was reluctant to answer the call. Turning over to sink deeper into the softness, she snuggled down and relaxed with a sigh.

"Is this the way you treat your friends?" the voice asked with humor. "Turning over and ignoring them?"

She sighed and flopped over upon her back. "I'm trying to sleep, here," she pouted, opening one eye.

Dark grey boots.

Kate bolted straight up and reached for her sword, but TinneHolm was nowhere to be found. Where was it?

Where was her sword?

"Do I honestly look like someone you would want to run through with a blade?"

The stranger was standing above Kate, hands on his hips, laughing down at her. He wore dark grey clothing, had silvery, shoulder-length hair and silvery blue eyes that sparkled with his smile. Silver and grey. Even his skin had a silvery tinge to it.

Kate's brows drew together and she moved her legs to a cross-legged position. "Who are you?" she asked, squinting up at him. She looked around at her surroundings, running a hand through her unbound hair, fingers catching at the ends. "And where am I?"

Wherever she was, Kate was sure she had never Walked to this world before. It was beautiful. She would definitely have remembered it. Seated under a huge tree with smooth brown bark warm against her back, she was in a sunny meadow. Light danced upon a small creek where dragonflies skimmed over water that tinkled musically through stones. Tiny white and yellow butterflies flitted over a meadow dotted with little yellow flowers. The grass was the bright green of early spring. The air was soft and perfumed with the fragrances of flowers and new growth.

Kate looked back at the man who had squatted down in front of her, forearms resting on his thighs, one side of his short cape rakishly tossed over his shoulder. He was lean and fit. She got the impression that he was a warrior.

"Who are you?" she repeated.

He waved the answer aside. "We'll get back to that. Tell me, Kate, how are you feeling?" Even with the slight wave of his hand, she could see he used no more energy than necessary. He moved like water. He was beautiful.

She looked at him, puzzled. "I feel great," she replied.

"Do you remember anything?"

Her eyes narrowed. "Should I?" she asked suspiciously.

The stranger threw back his head and laughed.

He nodded. "Yes, you should, Kate. You really should." The sparkle left his eyes. "Do you remember," he asked slowly, "your battle with the Searn?"

The Searn! Scattered images filled her mind. She sorted through them like puzzle pieces. Evil, sour husks. *Searn.* Eggs, glowing like marbles. Mog. Fighting using a shield. Why not fighting with TinneHolm? *TinneHolm! Blackened and broken!*

The pain shot through her heart once again. She clutched her chest with both hands, closing her eyes tight against the memories.

"I see that you do remember," the stranger said softly, kindly.

"TinneHolm, my Sword Ally—" Kate began.

"Ever at your service, Maiden."

Kate's eyes shot open. "Wh—?"

The man rose in one movement and presented a courtly bow. "I am he."

"Who?"

"TinneHolm, your Sword Ally. You are my Sword Maiden."

Kate's jaw dropped and she gaped at him.

"If you please, Maiden Kate, would you close your mouth? It detracts from your beauty."

Kate snapped her mouth shut and scowled.

"And the frown is not much of an improvement."

"Please sit down. You make me nervous standing up there," she said huffily, folding her arms and ignoring his comment.

"Ever at your service, Maiden," he repeated, and sat gracefully across from her, so close that their knees were touching.

Since she was up against a tree and couldn't move any further away, Kate endured the touch.

"You can't be TinneHolm."

"And why can I not?" he asked with a smile.

It was such a happy, genuine smile that Kate couldn't help but smile in return. "You're a man," she answered with a chuckle.

He reached out and touched her knee. "But I am TinneHolm, Kate, nonetheless."

Then Kate felt the connection. His touch *felt* like TinneHolm.

"You are," she agreed, soberly, "nonetheless." She paused, then continued. "And now I don't really know what to think other than I've finally gone crazy! How can my dead sword be sitting across from me?" Kate felt the blood draining from her face. Her eyes widened and she stared at TinneHolm. "Am I dead as well?" she whispered.

He looked sad. "You very nearly are, Kate," he answered, taking her hands in his. "I believe, at the moment, the choice is up to you."

She gasped. "But I don't want to die."

He reached out and captured a tear on his finger. "I know."

"What can I do?" she whispered.

"That, I do not know. But I am here, Kate, if that is some comfort, and I hope that it is," he replied with a small smile as he recaptured her hand.

She nodded and squeezed his hands, reassured when he returned the squeeze. She shook her bangs from her face. "So where are we?"

"Does it matter? We are here, of this I am glad, because I need to convey to you something very important," he said, adding, "while there is still time."

Kate nodded. "I'm listening."

He smiled. "You always do. I chose my Sword Maiden well when I selected you." He paused and smiled, his pleasure flowing through the connection they had created together.

"Now then, hear this, Kate. When I took the energy within me, fired from the Searn's weapon, I knew that it was too much and I would be destroyed. In that instant I made a decision. At the time,

I was not sure that it would work, but I see that it has." TinneHolm grinned. "Through our sword bond, I transferred everything that I am into you, Kate—my soul, my experience and my knowledge. You have it all."

TinneHolm paused to let the information settle into his Maiden.

"So," Kate began slowly, "I am two people? I am myself and I am also you?"

"Something like that. I am not sure if we can be separated from one another."

Kate thought it through. She had always felt that TinneHolm was a part of her and she a part of him, so the added information did not concern her so much.

Two souls, she mused.

Kate chuckled.

"Hey! I'm bi-souler!"

Her Sword Ally grinned. "No, I am," he retorted.

She laughed.

"So how will this work?" she asked after a pause.

"That I do not know."

"You won't try to take over, will you? Like some kind of demonic possession?"

As he felt all of her emotions, TinneHolm felt Kate's fear.

It hurt him.

"Why would I do that? This is your home, a home I have vowed to protect with my life. A home I *did* protect with my life. I regret that I invaded it, but I only did so because I do not want to die."

It was Kate's turn to hurt.

"Oh, TinneHolm, I'm so sorry I thought that." She let go of his hand and touched his face, looking deeply into his silvery eyes. "Please believe me."

He nodded. "It is a most unusual situation."

"These are unusual times," she answered, then continued with a soft chuckle. "I've been in so many unusual situations over the past couple of years that now the unusual has become the usual to me! So, this is just one more."

The sword nodded. "There is something more to tell you."

Kate waited.

"The dragon will attempt to heal my body and she will succeed. I believe she will also try to gift my mended body with new life. It will be a new soul, Kate, my twin to fit into my healed body. I do not know if it will accept you. But as my twin, it will accept me, so I will talk with it, and we will see what will be."

Kate gently let go of her Sword Ally's hands and rubbed her face. "This is all too confusing. If your twin accepts you, does that mean your soul will go back into the sword?"

TinneHolm shrugged. "I do not know. But, I do not think so."

"And if I die?"

TinneHolm shrugged again. "As in life, we will meet death as One. I am your Ally, Kate. Always." He leaned forward. "When the other Maidens died, I had to let them go, but with you!" He paused, his face wreathed with joy, "with you, Kate, that is not so."

Kate sighed, and ran a hand through her bangs, then smoothing them down. "I have to get this out in the open, here. You know I love Ash, right? That we're, like, married, right?"

TinneHolm laughed. He laughed louder when he saw her scowling, clutching his belly, his whole body shaking with laughter. He held up a hand. "I'm sorry, Kate, if I have offended you," he sputtered, managing to get the words out between fits of laughter. "Swords are not as humans. Never fear."

He paused while another bout of laughter overcame him. "I do appreciate that you think I am so beautiful that you felt compelled to say those words to me. I truly do, and I completely agree. I am beautiful. And I love you, Kate. I love you so much. If I could, I would die again and again for you. But I love as a sword loves." Continuing to laugh, he reached across and hugged her hard. "I love you as a sword loves," he repeated.

"Okay, *okaaay*!!" Kate replied, pushing him off her. "Now I'm embarrassed."

"No need," TinneHolm replied, with a grin. Then, he sobered. "The time is coming, Kate, for you to decide whether to live or to die."

"I want to live!" she replied without hesitation.

"I know you do, but once you regain consciousness, it may not be the case. Your body is in a lot of pain. The dragon is unsure if she can heal it. The pain may be too much."

"I need to try. I don't feel finished," Kate told the sword.

"I understand, and I wish you to live. Hear this now, Kate. Should you live, we will be able to communicate. You will know the difference in our thoughts. Perhaps you will even be able to see my spirit, I do not know. We will be learning together. Should you die, we will face that together as well. Ever after, from this time forward, we are united souls."

Kate felt a tugging and she looked at TinneHolm.

He nodded, saying, "It is time, My Sword Maiden. Go, and know I go with you."

She gave him a small smile then closed her eyes and lay down.

Chapter 11- Then Hope Again

Kate groaned.

"She's back!" Ash said to Clarion.

Tendrils of mist came over, touching Kate, exploring.

Ash had been sitting for so long, holding Kate in his lap, that his legs had grown numb. Wincing, he straightened them out. Kate groaned again, louder, with the movement.

Mog whined.

Ash glanced at the beast's ugly face, and his expression softened. After the dragon had healed the Battle Hound, Mog had immediately come over to lie down by Kate. The huge beast had not taken his eyes off of her since. Now, they flicked back and forth from Ash's face to Kate's and to the Ancient One's, as though he was trying to understand.

Moving TinneHolm aside, Ash rose to his knees and gently lay Kate flat on the floor of the cavern, once more using a shirt to cradle her head. He covered her with both his Walkers cloak and blanket, folding her blackened hands on the outside. Her hands were so very cold.

Out of the corner of his eye, Ash saw the sword shimmering with new life. Clarion had also healed TinneHolm. The combination of dragon fire and dragon magic had left Ash gasping. It had seemed so easy for her, so effortless, to mend the blade.

After the sword was healed, while they waited for Kate to regain consciousness, Clarion told Ash her story. She was about to explain the significance of all twelve Power Sources being alive when Kate had stirred.

Kate moaned and moved restlessly, her chalk-white face glistening with sweat.

Mog whined again and moved a little closer.

"There is still poison within her from the weapon." The dragon's thoughts flowed through Ash like smoke. *"I do not understand how it functions. It is burned into her hands and her shoulder. I pulled the poison out of my Battle Hound. I pulled it out of the sword when it was re-made. But I had no input in the making of this Maiden. It requires that I find a different way to work my healing magic."*

"But you will try, will you not?" Ash's usually calm voice cracked as he lovingly wiped Kate's face with a damp cloth. He reached for one of her blackened hands, stroking the lifeless fingers.

"I shall try, Ash of the Brendt. I do not wish to see this little one pass from this realm. There is need of such a one."

The dragon's bulk loomed over the prostrate girl. She bent down gracefully, tendrils of mist floated and swirled from her nostrils. *"Would you be able to sit her up? She could lean against my Hound."*

Mog's head lifted and he whined again, looking at Kate with troubled eyes as Ash propped her against the huge beast's side. Her head lolled back and she began to slide down. Ash scrambled to her and settled against the hound, his arm encircling Kate where she slumped against him, her head on Ash's shoulder. Tendrils of mist thickened over Kate's hands and shoulder wounds. When they cleared, her hands seemed brighter, her fingertips silver. Ash lifted one up to inspect it more closely.

"Her fingers appear as metal, yet they feel like skin," he said.

"The black was from the weapon. The silver is from something other than the wound. I cannot explain it. I have healed all that I can, Ash of the Brendt. Her life is in the balance. We will wait and see."

Ash stroked Kate's face with a fingertip, his eyes bright. "Kate," he whispered, "please come back to me, my heart, my Bond Mate." He drew her closer. "My heart is hurting so."

It took several minutes for Ash to realize that not only was his heart hurting, but there was a burning sensation. Without thinking he touched his chest where it hurt. He felt a lump, a very hot lump, in his breast pocket. The rock that Ioho had given him. "For boo-

boos" he had said. *Could it be so?* Ash removed the stone, finding it so hot that he had to juggle it a bit to keep it from burning him. As quickly as he could, he wrapped it in the cloth he had been using to wipe Kate's brow, his fingers fumbling in their haste. Thrusting the rock between Kate's hands, he closed his own over hers.

Kate screamed at the contact, and her eyes shot open, unseeing.

Ash flinched and tried to open her hands to remove the stone, but Kate would not let go. She held fast to the stone and screamed again. Her voice sounded hoarse and weak. There was a sizzling sound and the smell of burnt flesh rising from Kate's shoulder wound. Ash felt the bile rise in his throat.

Mog shifted and licked Kate's face.

"What is this?" The dragon's head loomed in Ash's peripheral vision. *"Earth magic, I believe. How did you come by it?"*

"Ioho gave it to me," Ash said distractedly, his eyes remaining glued to Kate. Her head began rolling side to side, her mouth in a grimace, and her eyes rolled so far back in her head that all Ash could see were the whites. Fear shot through him. "What is happening? Can you tell me, Ancient One? What is happening to my Kate?" His voice rose high as he tried to still her head. Her hands flashed silver where they gripped the stone.

114

"A battle is raging within her, Ash of the Brendt. She is the battlefield where the poison and the stone duel for her life. Take heart. She is strong. She has many reasons to choose life."

The Walker, the Hound and the dragon waited tensely until all became quiet and Kate relaxed with a sigh against Ash. Her hand loosened, and the once-pale stone slipped from the cloth, revealing that it had become as black as onyx. It shattered to dust when it hit the cave floor.

"It is done!" Clarion's thoughts rang with victory. *"The Sword Maiden has chosen life!"*

* * *

Kate regained conscious after having one last conversation with TinneHolm.

"I have talked with my twin," he said. "He needs us, Kate. He is so new. He has not even earned a name. For now, we shall call him Young Ally, and we will teach him all we know."

His words echoed in her head as she opened her eyes. She felt disoriented and confused, expecting to see TinneHolm's silvery face, but instead found Ash's beloved countenance gazing at her intently. Behind Ash loomed Mog's huge, ugly head. The Purp was grinning.

"Ash!" Her whole being lit up with joy. "I have missed you so much!"

"I have missed you as well," Ash said. "How do you feel, my Kate?" He was grinning as broadly, now, as the Battle Hound.

She grinned back, and reached up to stroke Ash's cheek. "You came for me!" She would have said more, but her fingertips caught her eye. She frowned, studying them, turning them this way and that. She held up her other hand. Those fingertips were just as silvery. She looked at Ash.

He shrugged, "Before you were healed, your hands were black.

"It looks permanent."

"Perhaps so."

"I suppose I will have to get used to them."

"I think they are rather lovely." Kate scowled. Not Clarion's voice in her head. TinneHolm's.

"If you are my permanent 'head guest,'" she thought forcefully, *"then we will have to set some rules. For now, please be quiet so I can focus and reunite with my Bond Mate."*

"Of course, I apologize. Let me add that I do believe the silver is the metal from my sword that merged with your flesh when I merged with your soul."

Kate nodded.

"I think your fingers are striking, my Kate. They are as unique as you are," Ash told her.

She smiled at him, and with his help, sat up to look around. Her eyes lit upon the tall columns. On top of each, one of twelve eggs was softly glowing.

"I did it!" she exclaimed. "Aren't they beautiful? Oh! Gross!"

Mog had managed to maneuver himself close enough to lick Kate's face enthusiastically and messily. Kate wiped her face with her arm and then gave the huge Hound a hug. "I'm happy to see you, too! You fought bravely, Mog. I was honored to fight beside you. And I am so glad you're healed."

She looked around.

"Where's Clarion?"

"The Ancient One went to the mouth of her cave to think," Ash replied.

"So she told you who she was."

"That she did, among other things."

Kate cocked an eyebrow.

"She will explain when she returns."

Ignoring her silver fingertips, Kate put her hands on Ash's face again. "Ash," was all she said.

117

He kissed her, holding her close.

Kate relaxed into the sound of his breathing and steady heartbeat.

"The Ancient One could heal her Battle Hound. She could heal your sword. But she could not heal you, my Kate. You nearly died again."

There was a catch in his throat.

Kate nodded against his chest. Her arms tightened around Ash. "I know. Those weapons they had…," she shook her head. "The Searn? They were pure evil, Ash. They don't want to just kill their enemies. They want their enemies to die in agony. When TinneHolm died, I went crazy. I wanted to kill every single one of them. But there were too many. And Mog was wounded.

Because of me. I will *not* watch another of my comrades die, like Tinneholm did, because of me! And, here I go again, rambling. Time to kick it."

"Ioho knew what would happen."

"Huh?" Kate drew back to look at Ash's face. "Joey knew?"

"He gave me a stone when I said good-bye to him." Ash's lips curved into a smile. "Said it was for boo-boos. I thought nothing of it until it began to heat up in my pocket when I held you close. I put it in your hands. The stone drew out the poisons. That is how you were made whole."

118

"Wow, Joey knew," Kate repeated, shaking her head. "What an amazing little boy he is."

"That is so. Truly."

"Ash, we can't say anything about this."

"Why remain silent?"

"Joey's on such a pedestal as it is, being the savior of all of Ruis, harbinger of the golden age, and all that. If the Kinsmen learn all he can do, he will have no childhood. He'll be looked at as some freak, a good freak and wonderful and all…but still a freak, and the poor little guy won't even be allowed to be a wonderful kid. He's only two years old!"

Ash was quiet for several moments before he answered. "I did not think of that. I believe that you could be correct in this."

"He has to live like us, be like us…be a part of us to lead us, don't you see? He has be one of us in order to understand us, and the Kinsmen need to accept him as one of us so that they will trust him and allow him to lead them." She wiggled her silver fingertips at Ash. "Just like I have to see beneath these silvery guys and accept them as my own."

Ash caught her hands, kissing her fingers. "I agree with you, my Kate. You can stop trying to convince me."

119

Kate laughed and hugged Ash hard. "I was so scared, Ash. I thought I'd never see you again."

His arms tightened around her. "I was terrified as well. Sword Maiden or not, we stay together from now on."

"Walker or not. We stay together," she replied.

Mog whined and Kate laughed. "Purp-Eye or not, Mog, we stay together."

Mog grinned and thumped his tail.

Kate sighed. "I need to tell you about TinneHolm, and I need to eat something. Do you have any food, Ash? I dumped all my stuff out of my pack to make room for the eggs."

"Clarion created a feast for us, my Kate. Look here."

Kate sat up, her eyes widening at the sight of a platter heaping with dried fruit, nuts, bread and meats. "Where did *that* come from? This place is a wasteland."

Ash grinned. "'This is the First World, the home of the First People. All things are possible with my Power Source restored to me.'"

Kate giggled and punched Ash in the arm. "You sound just like her," she said, reaching for a handful of the dried fruit and nut mixture.

As they ate, Kate told Ash about her Sword Ally.

"And so you have become a weapon yourself, Kate."

Kate nodded thoughtfully. "I guess I have. I'm half me and half sword, I suppose." She shook her head. "It's going to take some getting used to."

"To be sure," Ash agreed after a moment.

"What is it?"

Ash looked at her, questioningly.

"Something is bothering you, I can tell. What is it?" Kate repeated.

"I do not like that another has claim over your attention," he confessed.

Kate nodded her understanding. "And if TinneHolm were within you, I don't think I'd like it either. But it's not like TinneHolm's a person. He's a sword, you know? It's just the same as his being within a sword body, only he can't get back into it anymore, so he's stuck inside me. But I still make the choices. When he was a sword, unless my life was endangered, I chose when to draw him out and fight. I still have the same control. Does that make sense?"

"Aye, Kate, it does. But I can tell you are different."

121

She wiggled her silver fingertips at him. "Ya think? What gave it away?" she asked, trying to lighten the mood. When she saw Ash smile, she relaxed a little. "Listen, I fight with my sword, and I can't lie that I'm not curious to see where this new relationship with it will take me. But I chose you as my Bond Mate. I want you, Ash, and nobody else. Not ever. Please believe me." She held Ash's gaze.

When he reached for her, she relaxed completely. "I believe you," he said into her hair.

Mog *woofed* softly, and they reluctantly drew apart, listening.

Chapter 12 - The Power Source or the Dragon?

Kate immediately heard the difference as the Ancient One came down through the lava tube. Her footfalls seemed lighter, as though it was easier for her to move. She sounded younger. Kate craned her neck so she could see Clarion as soon as her head came into light. The telltale wisps of fog came first, and then there she was.

Kate gasped, slowly rising to her feet, Ash and Mog following her lead.

She had thought the dragon beautiful before, but now, with the Power Source back where it belonged, she was absolutely stunning. The greens, blues and purples were enhanced and brilliant, and they shimmered and flowed with each breath that Clarion took. Kate looked at the other eggs, high on their pedestals, and imagined what twelve dragons must have been like. And to ride on one! Now *that* would be so awesome!

Clarion paused in front of Kate, flaring her frill. She arched her neck and swung her head gracefully down to the two Walkers. And then she bowed low with her head touching a foreleg.

"I am extremely joyful that you have survived, Sword Maiden. With deep humility I tell you I am honored to know one such as yourself," the Ancient One said. *"You have returned hope to the First World."*

At a loss for words, Kate waited for the dragon to unfold from her bow before answering. "I did what had to be done," she said simply, still surprised that one as ancient and noble as Clarion would actually bow to her!

"And you nearly ceased to exist. I will forever be indebted to you and your loved ones. If you ever have need of me, I will be honored to serve you."

Kate bowed her head, overwhelmed. She reached out, her silver fingertips touching the dragon's muzzle.

"You have changed much, young one."

Kate nodded. "I have. TinneHolm lives inside me. His soul bonded with mine."

"Ahhh, that ends the puzzle. When I healed your sword for you, I could only sense the shadow of its essence. And now you are a true Sword Maiden. You do not need a weapon to make you thus."

Kate smiled, looking at her fingertips. "I guess so. I never thought of it that way. We, TinneHolm and I, want to train the sword you healed."

"A worthy aspiration. I am certain the sword will be very grateful to you."

The dragon swung her elegant head towards Ash.

"Your Bond Mate loves you very much, Maiden. He did not leave your side once, although he has obligations that call to him.

Kate reached for Ash's hand as the dragon whispered through their minds, and she smiled at him. "And now that I'm well, we probably should get back to those obligations."

They both sensed a reluctance in the dragon.

"Maiden, might I impose upon you one more time? I have a need."

Kate's eyes widened. "A need?" She glanced at Ash.

He shook his head, shrugging.

"What is your need, Ancient One?" Kate asked.

"As you were healing, I was pondering. The life within the other Power Sources was unexpected. It was assumed that when the Company gifted their lives to me, their Power Sources would cease to exist as well.

Kate felt Clarion's shiver of joy rush through her own body.

"But how wrong we were! And now, I have the opportunity to re-gift their lives in return."

"How?" Ash asked.

"The answer to your question, Walker, is that I am unsure. As I stand before you, I am unable. My body is too ancient. I will need to re-birth myself."

The Ancient One turned her attention once more to Kate.

"This is where I will have a great need, for you see I am the only one who remains. There is a period of seven days when I will be very vulnerable. If the Company were whole, one of us would stand guard. I am asking you, Sword Maiden, to fill in for my missing companions and guard me for those seven days."

Kate glanced at Ash, who nodded.

"I can do that for you," Kate said. "If you could wait a little, I would like to help Ash relocate our Kinsmen. But, when that is done, I will be able to help you." Kate paused. "I want to help you."

The dragon inhaled and then exhaled in one long sigh, loosening tendrils of mist that snaked around Kate. *"I am deeply grateful, Maiden, but before I accept your promise, there is more.*

"During those seven days, the First World will be without the leadership of the First People. I do not know what will happen. The portals will be unguarded. There will be no guarantee that unwanted ones such as the Searn will not slip through. No, they will not be the Searn, the Searn will never be able to reach the

First World now what I destroyed that last portal. But there are always uninvited others who could happen in."

"But what about Mog and the other Battle Hounds?" Kate asked. "Won't they be guarding the trees?"

"Without my control, I cannot be sure that the Battle Hounds will remain loyal."

Kate looked sharply at Mog, who thumped his tail and moved closer to Kate.

"Even Mog?"

"Perhaps Mog will remain loyal, as he has become rather attached to you, Maiden. That is yet another reason I ask this of you. I am at a dangerous crossroads with few options and many unknowns. I am too weak to share my life force with the Company, although I am stronger than I have been in centuries.

"If I do nothing, I will eventually die, and my dilemma will be the same as before you returned our Power Sources, except that I have purchased perhaps another two to three hundred years. No more than that. Not long at all."

Kate nodded to herself. "Not long at all, if you are used to being immortal."

"There is a strong connection between the First World and the First People. As you have not exited my nest, you cannot see the

changes since the return of my Power Source. When you do, imagine what it will be when I am young again. Then, imagine further when the Company is returned."

Clarion flared her frill. Steam burst from her nostrils, causing Ash and Kate to take a step back.

"I am unused to the unknown. In the thousands of years that I have witnessed and lived, there has never been such a time as this. It is either an end or a beginning, and I am unclear as to which."

"Perhaps it is both," suggested Ash, his hand on Kate's shoulder.

"Perhaps so, Walker."

Kate absently wound her fingers in Mog's silky ruff. "I will help you, Ancient One," Kate finally said. "I think you need to rebirth yourself. If you can give us the time to settle our Kinsmen and ensure that they are all safe, then I will be free to come back."

"As will I," said Ash.

Kate glanced at him. "But don't you think our Kinsmen will need a Walker?"

Ash shook his head, "I will not leave you again to face dangers alone. Never again," he repeated.

Kate felt his hand on her shoulder tighten, and she smiled in relief and joy. "Thank you," she said leaning against him. "Never again, Ash..."

"I can give you time. I need to prepare as well. I sustain my Battle Hounds and the guardians of the stone portals. Without me, they will go hungry. Pack will attack pack, and they will devour one another."

Kate shuddered. "How many are there?"

"Not many. I have created three hundred Hounds. More, I could not sustain."

Ash and Kate glanced at one another. "I think three hundred of these guys is plenty." Kate said.

"I have created a portal for you, Walker and Maiden. It is at the mouth of my nest. It will be guarded well, so have a care when you return. My Hounds have your scent, but errors can happen.

Kate looked at Ash. "I guess we should get ready to leave?"

"Upon your return, please bring yourself provisions for seven days. And one other thing: I ask you tell no one what I am or what you have seen until I have rebirthed myself. Placing my trust into your hands has made me feel vulnerable, I have never given humans power over my life before, and placing my trust in you is difficult.

"I must warn you that I will protect myself. My life and the life of the Company are my highest priority."

"It is understood," replied Ash.

"We will tell no one." Kate paused. "Ancient One, there is a Wise Woman, if I could tell her about the connection between the First People and the First World," she blurted out, "maybe she could tell me what to expect in these seven days?"

The dragon arched her neck, snaking her head, frill flaring.

"Have a care what you say, Maiden. I will protect myself. You have crossed the wasteland. You know what can be done. I choose to keep myself in the First World. I do not have to remain here."

Kate made a patting motion with her hands. "I did not mean to upset you. She may not be as old as you, but she is wise, and she understands the connection between people and their land. I thought to be more prepared, is all."

"Understood, Maiden. I know you mean no harm. I know you will protect me. I am unused to trusting those not of my making and outside of the Company. I am unused to having allies."

Kate surprised herself when she went down on one knee. With a fist over her heart, she bowed low. "With all that I am, Ancient One, I vow to protect you."

Following her lead, Ash knelt and made his own vow. They stayed where they were as tendrils of mist flowed around them.

"Understood, accepted, and appreciated."

* * *

Kate and Ash stood on the ridge overlooking the three valleys deep in the wilderness of Ruis.

"It is so beautiful!."

"That it is, my Kate," Ash agreed. "It is also where I left Lorcan and two scouts."

"Can you sense a trail?"

"I am attempting to do so."

Kate was silent, allowing Ash the time he needed.

She took a deep breath, soaking up the beauty of the vista. Forest and mountains spread before her. Ash had pointed out to her the three sites for the proposed encampments. She liked how they were close together, but far enough apart that they could each be defended. It looked like a perfect place to live, and easy to defend.

She was feeling surprised that she could see all that by just looking about and studying the ridge lines, when it suddenly occurred to her that TinneHolm was supplying her with the information. *"I know more of the art of war than just swordplay,"* her Ally whispered into her mind. Kate nodded absently, realizing that, with their blended souls, she had become a powerful asset for the Brendt. Her heart thrilled.

"I am finding nothing," Ash said. "Perhaps in the two or so days we have been gone they have returned to our encampment."

Kate nodded. "It makes sense."

She let Ash lead them home. They stepped out of the quiet and into the noise of a disembarking camp.

"There they are!" someone shouted.

"Walker!" shouted another. "Brann told us to send ye to him as soon as ye turned up."

Ash nodded a thank you, and the two went in search of their leader.

They found him in the midst of an argument with Lady Faith and Lorcan.

"Who is the Leader of our Clan, I'm askin ya?" he shouted, face red, a vein throbbing at his temple. "Now go about it!" Brann turned and saw them. "It's about time," he snarled. "We were about to set off over land."

"And now there is no need," Ash replied calmly.

Kate, standing quietly, flicked her braid to her back nervously as she waited for instructions. She'd never attempted to Walk such a huge group at once.

Faith's welcoming smile was replaced with a look of surprise and curiosity when her glance caught the flicker of silver.

"Kate!" she exclaimed. "Your hands.

"Kate looked ruefully down at her fingertips."Yup. It's permanent."

"Are you well, my dear?"

"Yes, better than ever." Kate grinned.

Brann glanced at Kate's hands. "I suspect there is quite a tale you'll be telling."

"Indeed," said Kate, glancing at Ash. "But it will need to wait."

"Kate has another task, and I will be accompanying her this time," he said with steely resolve. "We have only returned long enough to aid our Kinsmen with the move and then gather supplies."

Brann and Lorcan nodded. Walkers were a strange breed, with their comings and goings. They knew Ash was loyal and could be counted on to keep his word, and it was enough. But Kate could tell by the look she gave that Faith was not going to let it rest. Even though she remained silent, Kate knew she'd be cornered and questioned by the Wise Woman as soon as there was a moment of calm. She smiled.

In the meantime, Ash joined Brann and Lorcan in developing a strategy for the most efficient relocation of the Kinsmen.

None saw the cloaked figure flattened to the side of a tree, hidden within the dappled shadows.

Chapter 13 - Birth and Death

It had taken them nearly two weeks to move the encampment. Kate had never been more exhausted in her life, both mentally and physically. It took a huge amount of concentration to keep the portals open for the wagons of people and supplies. Depending upon the size of the caravans, they could manage about three to four loads a day. At night, she and Ash would stumble off to bed, barely keeping their eyes open long enough to eat and to visit with Joey.

Kate didn't need a sword summoning to feel the dragon's urgency and, by osmosis, neither did Ash.

"The Ancient One grows impatient, does she not?" he asked one night, near the end of the move, as they lay together in their tent.

Kate stifled a yawn. "I'm feeling torn in two," she answered, "I can't wait until it's just you and me and Joey. I miss it."

"As do I, my Kate, as do I," he answered, pulling her closer and stroking her hair.

"I haven't even been able to thank him for saving my life," she mumbled.

"He knows how you feel, Kate."

She nodded against Ash's chest. "Probably, but I still need to thank him."

The mists were thicker than usual in the Place-Between-Worlds, but Kate often caught glimpses of purple eyes. Now that she knew about the Battle Hounds, she was glad that they were there watching and protecting the portals.

Finally, the move was completed. Kate and Ash didn't wait for the Kinsmen to settle into their new encampments. They gathered their things, packing a crate with ten days' worth of food and water. In their packs they had their clothing. When they were ready to leave, they searched out Brann and Faith.

"I've not had a chance to speak with you," the Wise Woman told Kate, "but I feel something has changed between you and your Sword Ally."

"You could say that," Kate said with a slight smile. "I had some questions to ask you as well, but it doesn't look like I've the time. I'm being summoned again, you see."

"By the Ancient One?"

Kate nodded. "When I can, I will tell you all I know."

Faith smiled. "I do hate being kept in the dark," she said with a laugh. She reached out and gave the young woman a quick hug. "Take good care of yourself, my Sword Sister. You seem to have a knack for placing yourself in harm's way."

Kate hugged her back, "Thanks. I'm just glad that Joey is safe, and I've got Ash with me this time. We shouldn't be gone more than ten days."

"Thank you both for your skills," Brann said, shaking his head. "In truth, I did not know what I was asking when I requested that you Walk us through."

Ash and Kate waved good-bye and went to find Joey.

He was waiting for them, standing apart from the group of playing children, with a serious expression on his little face.

Kate scooped him up, "I love you so much, Prince Boy!" she exclaimed, feeling his little arms wrapping themselves around her neck. "If it wasn't important, we wouldn't be leaving so soon. I promise, when we come back, we will have plenty of time to be together." She hugged him to her. "Oh, Joey, I will miss you."

Joey handed her a pebble. "Find me," he said with a small smile, toying with her silver fingertips.

136

She tucked the pebble away. "I can always find you with my heart, Joey," she said, handing him to Ash.

Not wanting to let go, she hugged them both.

With a sigh, Ash set Joey down and led Kate to the nearest tree. "We're going to go to the portal at Clarion's cave," he told her, taking her hand in a promise, a bond, that had nothing to do with safely finding their way through the Place-Between-Worlds.

Kate nodded. With one backward glance at Joey, she stepped through with Ash.

* * *

Clarion was waiting for them, surrounded by Mog's pack of Battle Hounds. Mog let out a *woof* and licked Kate's face before she could protect herself from his slobbery tongue. With a laugh, she scratched his broad forehead before nudging him aside.

Kate glanced around, noticing new growth greening the valley floor. She thought she saw the outline of a deer, but wasn't sure. One of Clarion's preparations to nourish the Hounds?

"Welcome, and thank you, Maiden and Walker. I am prepared. Are you as well?" The dragon's familiar resonance swept through their minds. Kate sensed a deep sadness and wondered why.

She and Ash nodded in unison.

"I would ask the two of you to remain outside to guard the nest's mouth. However, I have concern for the Searn portal. I believed it to be closed forever. Destroyed. But the longer I muse upon the subject, the more uncertain I have become. Mog and his Hounds will guard the mouth."

The dragon paused, and again Kate sensed sadness.

"I have no desire for you to witness my rebirth. It is a painful and ugly process, a secret kept long within the Company. But I can see no way around this dilemma if I am to be assured of my safety during my vulnerability. Therefore, let us begin and hasten through this ill event. You will need a light source."

Kate and Ash picked up their supply crate and followed the dragon down through the tube into the huge cavern. Even in the translucent light, Kate could see that little had changed since their last visit. Ash led Kate over to where her shield was propped against the cavern's wall. They put their supply crate down beside it. From where they stood, they had a clear view of the center of the columns, the now-closed Searn portal.

"Shall we set up our camp?" Kate asked.

Ash nodded, "That we shall, my Kate."

They brought out their bedrolls and made a place to sleep. Ash had also thought to bring a couple of sling-back folding chairs, and they created a little sitting area near their bedding.

From her pack Kate produced a propane lantern, two extra canisters of propane, and a lighter. Ash lifted an eyebrow, and Kate shrugged at him as she placed the lantern on the crate. Walkers were not allowed to bring things from other worlds, although many did. Kate had decided that since she wasn't from Ruis, their rules didn't apply her.

The dragon said with humor, *"I have always admired how your peoples could make nests wherever they chose."*

"We're ready, Ancient One," Kate said.

"Then I shall begin. Please stay in the background and make no effort to intervene, despite what you may see. Is this clear to you both?

"Yes," Kate answered, adding, "I am sorry that it has to be this way. You have our word that we will never speak of this to anyone."

The dragon bowed her head. *"I thank you, Maiden, for your assurances."*

Ash drew Kate down beside him in their chairs. They both drew their swords and lay them across their laps, ready to protect the dragon if necessary.

C. B. Williams

The dragon was right. The rebirthing process was not pretty, although it began that way. The beautiful dragon lifted her brilliantly glowing egg with her magic. It floated at the dragon's eye level, a glowing orb of swirling color. Tenderly, she breathed her dragon fire. As the fire caressed the egg, it began to pulse, as if a heartbeat was growing stronger within it. Clarion's colors swirled and danced in the space between the floating egg and the Ancient One. As the colors organized themselves, they formed an energy pattern—an energetic highway—in the shape of an infinity symbol, the colored lights flashing and reflecting off the cavern's walls. Back and forth the colors moved, and all the while the egg expanded and pulsed to the heartbeat.

"Oh, wow," breathed Kate, a half-smile on her face.

"Aye," whispered Ash beside her.

When the egg reached a certain size, it began tearing and stretching. Suddenly it burst apart, the leathery shell disintegrating in the dragon fire. Hovering in its place was a miniature Clarion, no more than a foot long from head to tail-tip. With a shrill cry the tiny dragon darted like a spear and buried itself into the heart of its parent, a tiny blur of death.

There was a pause. It probably lasted for less than a second, but to Kate it was a memory that she would carry for the rest of her life.

Ash had felt it, too. She knew because, in the instant right before that significant pause, they looked at each other.

One moment they were staring into each other's eyes and the next moment—during the pause—they simply did not exist, as if they were drawings on a chalkboard that someone had erased. Nothing.

Except, they did exist on some level, because they were aware that they were nothing, unmade, just the memory of who they were. No, not even a memory. Simply nothing. And that part of themselves that did exist on some level had just learned that they could so easily be turned into nothing, even with all the life that they felt flowing through them and with all their plans, goals and dreams. That knowledge filled them with a terror that went beyond words.

And then the moment passed and they were back, staring into each other's eyes.

Ash had gone white.

Kate saw the same terror in his eyes that she felt.

They were reaching for each other when Clarion roared in agony and collapsed onto the cavern floor, tail whipping as she bucked and writhed in pain. Even before the light died from the lovely golden eyes, the little one emerged in a spray of blood with Clarion's still-pumping heart, and proceeded to devour it in loud gulps. The steaming meat slid down the young one's throat and it cried out in hunger and pleasure. Then it retreated back into the dying dragon for more food.

Ash had grabbed Kate by her arm as she stood to defend the Ancient One.

"Remember, do not interfere."

With a whimper, Kate sat back. "It's too late anyway," she said, swallowing hard.

Outside, she heard the Battle Hounds howl.

Suddenly it went dark, the sounds of chewing, tearing and gulping assaulted their ears. The warm stench of blood and organs filled the large cavern. Kate covered her mouth to keep from retching.

"God, it's worse with the lights out, Ash."

"Aye, that it is. Give me but a moment," he replied, and Kate could hear him fumbling with the lighter she'd placed by the lantern. The smell of propane mingled with that of offal. The light revealed that Clarion was now no more than a carcass, the young dragon still feeding enthusiastically.

"Ugggggh," Kate said, reaching for Ash's hand again, her fingertips glinting in the lantern light.

For three days and three nights Kate and Ash took turns standing guard as the little dragon feasted upon its parent, its belly bloated with each meal. When Clarion's remains were nearly devoured, the young one heaved a great sigh, curled up like a cat, and slept by its kill, oblivious to its surroundings.

The hiss of the propane lantern was the only sound.

Kate looked at Ash.

"Do you think we should put out some Walker feelers to explore that portal?" Ash asked, nodding his head in the direction of the columns.

"Good idea," Kate replied. "You do it. You're better at it than I am."

Kate stood beside Ash, Young Ally in her hand, and watched as he tested the portal.

"Look!" she whispered. "Whenever you touch it, the other eggs get brighter. Do you think they are guarding the opening?"

"Aye, it appears to be so. The portal is closed. I can find no weakness."

Kate sighed. "That's a relief. I really don't want to fight the Searn again. Ash, they come like rats. Relentless. And those laser sticks! Horrible and evil things."

"You brought one with you in your fist. I had to wrestle it from your grip."

Kate shuddered. "What happened to it?"

"It was destroyed by dragon fire."

"Good!" she exclaimed vehemently.

"While it is quiet, should we dine at last?" Ash asked.

As long as the little dragon had been awake and feeding, neither had had much of an appetite.

Kate opened her mouth to reply when a volley of barking and deep growls came from the mouth of the cave, followed by the sounds of fighting. Kate and Ash ran to the tube's entrance and peered up. It was as pitch dark outside as it was within. There was a high, keening cry, and then silence.

"*Mog!*" Kate shouted.

A deep growl answered her shout. Purple eyes glowed out of the darkness. The growl sounded again. Kate looked wildly at Ash, gripping her sword. She sent a questioning thought to TinneHolm's soul within her. *"Give the beast a command. It is frightened and needs direction."*

"Mog, come," Kate ordered, putting all her will behind the summons.

The purple eyes glowed brighter as they came closer. Ash tried to push Kate behind him.

"No, it's okay, Ash. Trust me."

She sensed his reluctance as he moved to stand next to her.

Mog whined when he reached the mouth of the tube. His nostrils flared at the scent of death.

"It's okay, Mog," Kate said gently and firmly. "Come to me."

He stood in front of her, trembling and uncertain. There was blood on his muzzle. Kate handed her sword to Ash so that she could hug the beast. "You poor thing," she crooned. "You can't hear Clarion in your head anymore, can you, boy? You're doing a great job guarding the portals. What a good Hound! The best Battle Hound ever."

Mog wagged his tail and whined again.

"You're my brave Battle Hound, aren't you, Mr. Purp? It's okay," Kate said, patting and stroking the big animal until he licked her face. "Ack! Okay! I can tell you're feeling better," she said. "Now, back you go. No more fighting amongst yourselves, Mog. You and your pack must guard the portal."

Mog *woofed* and trotted back up the tube to the lip of the cave, guarding the little sapling that Clarion had grown for Ash and Kate to use as a portal.

Kate looked at Ash, "I know that Mog's the strongest, but I just hope he doesn't have to prove it to his pack over and over again." She shivered, remembering the sounds of their fighting.

"We can only hope, my Kate," Ash replied, putting an arm around her waist, "But your talk with him seems to have given him a renewed purpose."

* * *

For three more days the dragon slept, growing bigger in front of their eyes.

"This is just like watching a time-lapse camera!" Kate whispered.

"A what?"

"Umm, how to describe this? Something that records images of an event that takes a long time and then plays it back really fast. Like a rose opening up," Kate explained using her hands to show a blossoming rose.

Ash nodded, and they watched the dragon grow another foot.

"This is just like watching a time-lapse camera," Ash told Kate without taking his eyes off the dragon.

She punched him in the shoulder.

They sat and talked in quiet whispers as they guarded their sleeping charge, taking turns sleeping themselves. On the sixth day, Ash noticed that it was getting lighter. As he stood guard, Kate ventured outside. Mog sat up and thumped his tail when he saw her, and she stroked his head. The land seemed to shimmer with a different light, brighter than the translucent glow of the Place-Between-Worlds Kate was used to. The air smelled sweeter, too, a soft breeze carrying the scents of new growth. *An actual breeze!*

Kate glanced around at the other Battle Hounds, realizing that one was gone. Eaten, perhaps by the others? Kate decided she didn't really want to know.

With an inner lift of hope , she gave Mog one last pat and returned to report to Ash, accepting the water flask he offered her.

"It smells so fresh out there," she whispered.

They sat and ate a meal in silence, watching the dragon sleep.

"Did I not say it was an ugly process?" The familiar voice swirled through their minds.

Ash and Kate jumped to their feet.

"Clarion!"

"Ancient One!"

One golden eye opened, tinged with humor.

"It feels good to be young again!"

"Are you truly back?" Kate asked. "Can you remember everything?"

"Of course I can, Maiden! And the time of my vulnerability has nearly come to an end. All that is left is to shed my skin. I need to feed once more, and my skin will be shed while I sleep."

The dragon lifted her head and looked about her, her eyes resting first on the other eggs glowing steadily upon their pedestals.

"All is well?

"Everything is just fine," Kate replied. "We tested the portal and we think that the other...um...Power Sources were guarding it as well."

"Indeed? How very fascinating."

The young dragon stood and stretched. She was quick and lithe, her colors brighter, and they sparkled as she opened her wings, testing their strength.

"I am anxious to fly. It has been nearly five hundred years since I last flew."

Kate looked excitedly at Ash, his eyes as bright as her own. "We would love to see you fly. I bet you are beautiful."

The dragon nodded. *"I am very beautiful. Now, please excuse me while I finish my rebirthing process."*

She returned to the last of the remains of her old body and settled down to feed once more with enthusiasm.

Kate made a face as Clarion began crunching on the bones. "It's not as bad, though, knowing that Clarion is back in her new body."

They watched the dragon eat the rest of her old body. When she was finished, nothing remained. Without any communication to Kate and Ash, she once more curled up and went to sleep.

When she next woke, there was a dragon-sized skin and a new egg where the old one had been.

Chapter 14 - Eaeda

Apparently, Mog the Battle Hound had switched loyalties. When Kate and Ash crossed back into Ruis, Mog was at Kate's side.

Kate put down the shield Clarion had insisted she take and stood with her hands on her hips. "Mog! What are you doing here?" she demanded.

Mog sat, grinned, and cocked his head, waiting expectantly.

She glanced worriedly at Ash. "What do you think?"

"I would not try to argue with a Battle Hound," Ash said with a grin which turned into a grimace as the large beast slathered his face with is slobbery tongue.

Laughter bubbled up from Kate. "Then he stays," she said.

"I'm happy to have you with me," she told the Hound.

The Purp grinned and tried to lick Kate as well, but she managed to duck in time to avoid another face bath.

The thought of a hot meal made Kate's stomach gurgle. "Let's get to camp, shall we?" Picking up her shield, she began to trot towards their new encampments, backpack thumping to the rhythm of her gait.

With a laugh, Ash joined her while Mog sped on ahead.

"What shall we do with this dragon skin?" Kate asked as they jogged along.

Clarion had also given them the skin that she had shed to complete the rebirthing process. When Kate had touched it, she was surprised at how soft and supple it had been. She had assumed it would be dry and papery like discarded snake skin.

"Skin from an immortal dragon? Protective clothing, of course."

Kate nodded. "Good idea. I doubt much can penetrate dragon skin."

Mog *woofed* a warning, and they drew to a halt, straining over their breathing to hear what the Hound had heard.

In the distance, they made out faint cries of alarm.

They looked at one another and broke into a run, Mog racing ahead at twice their speed.

"Wait Ash!" Kate shouted, stopping short and flinging off her pack. "Mog, come back!" she called.

The Hound turned and came racing back.

Kate scrambled onto his broad back and offered a hand towards Ash who had already thrown his pack on top of her own. "Watch my shield's edges," she warned him as he swung up behind her. "Go, Mog!" she commanded when they were ready.

The Battle Hound charged up the path and into the middle of the first Brendt encampment. Shouts and screams greeted their arrival.

Seeing Faith with her Sword Ally drawn, Kate leaped off Mog and headed towards her, calling her name. Faith turned and her eyes widened, taking in Kate's shimmering shield and the huge Hound with the glowing eyes that Ash rode. She opened her mouth but no sound came out at first. "Well, this is more than a surprise," she told Kate lamely.

"What's happened?" Kate asked. Ash dismounted from Mog to stand by Kate.

"It's Lofpht! They took Joey!"

"What?" Rage consumed Kate, a rage so huge she could barely contain it. *"So this is how a sword loves,"* she thought.

"It is, indeed," TinneHolm answered with icy determination.

"When?" Kate asked Faith in a tone just as icy as TinneHolm's.

"Moments ago."

"Ash?" Kate said.

But Ash was already sensing for a trail.

Kate felt a hand on her sleeve. "Kate? What have you become?" She heard fear laced with awe in the words Faith had spoken.

Eyes upon Ash, following his movements, Kate answered in a voice not quite her own, "I am Eaeda, the Shield. And soon, Lophft will know to fear me and my Battle Hound." Something burned in her pocket, and she pulled out the pebble Joey had given her. *Find me,* he had told her. "Lophft is about to be very, very sorry, I can promise you that. Ash!" She called and dashed over to her Bond Mate, handing him the pebble. "Joey gave this to me before we left for the rebirthing."

Their eyes locked and Ash nodded once.

"Mog!" Kate called. "We Walk."

She took Ash's outstretched hand, grabbed a fistful of Mog's fur, and followed Ash through the portal he had just opened.

* * *

"Why hand me the child?" whined Spindle Slan, Council Member of Lophft, rubbing his nose, the nose that had just been twisted by an angry two-year-old. "Have Estelle hold him. She's the woman here." His voice echoed against the high walls of the Council Room Chambers.

"Estelle cannot hold him," Estelle said, continuing to speak of herself in the third person, "because Estelle is holding the sword with which she will slay him." She turned toward the Walker standing quietly to the side. "You did well, my dear. I thank you for helping me to avenge my son's death."

AnnWyn nodded. "I did it for Straif," she said quietly. There was a time that she would have refused to turn an innocent child over to those who wanted to slay him, especially since it was said that the boy was The-One-Who-Brings-Peace. But her peace had died when she had seen the man she loved die.

Watching Straif's brother come bursting through the portal on that day, taking the Sword Maiden and the baby, while leaving his own brother to bleed out alone in a foreign land had irrevocably changed the Walker. Then and there, she had vowed to bring the House of Brendt down, and to do all she could to avenge Straif's death.

"Silence, Spindle!" Ogdan, the Elder said. For such a slight man, the Head Council member had a powerful voice. "Just hold him until we are readied. The boy is a King and deserves the respect of a King's death. We are not barbarians."

"Here," said Col Ailim reaching out his arms, "Let me take the lad. I understand them."

It was the last thing he ever said.

The door of the Council Chambers slammed open and a woman whose eyes shone with the same glint of silver as her fingertips came striding into the room with a Walker and growling creature close behind. Using the shield on her arm, she removed the head of Col Ailim from his shoulders.

Before Col's body hit to the ground, the woman was already focused upon Spindle Slan. She approached him with purposeful strides.

Slan squeaked and dropped the toddler king into the waiting grasp of the warrior woman.

She hadn't even unsheathed her sword.

In the silence, she scanned each of their faces as they tried not to stare at the shield dripping with Col Ailim's blood. From behind her a growl, so deep that it reverberated in the chests of all standing within the room, sprang from the throat of a monstrously large beast.

"Stand down, Mog," the woman said quietly. "I see no warrior worthy to be your meal here."

She turned to go, but paused in the silence, child on her hip. "Hear this!" Her voice was as sharp as the blade by her side. "I am Eaeda The Shield, Sword Maiden and Sword-Souled. Wherever Ioho goes, there, too, will be his Shield." she said, quoting from the Book of Phagos.

She turned, and, without a backward glance, exited the chambers, Battle Hound and Bond Mate on either side.

Through the open doors, those remaining in the room looked at the devastation the warrior woman had left behind her.

155

"I do believe we are finally at war," Ogdan, the Elder murmured with a steely glint in his eye. "Prophecy or no prophecy, the Brendt are doomed."

THE END

C.B. Williams lives on five acres in the Northern California redwoods with her husband, son, two dogs, five cats and the wild things that share their space with her.

When she's not writing or being a manuscript midwife, you can find her either painting, playing or adventuring.

C.B. has a black belt in Kashima Shin Ryu, where she learned that a black belt is just the very beginning.

Coming in 2013:   The Shield, Book Three of the Walkers Trilogy

Haven't read WALKERS? Just go to her website for the link!

Enjoying the Walkers Trilogy?   C.B. loves to hear from her readers, so feel free to contact her.

Website: www.2inspire.us

Email:cbw@2inspire.us

www.ingramcontent.com/pod-product-compliance
Lightning Source LLC
Chambersburg PA
CBHW070927130626
46555CB00001B/323